Novels
by ANDREW GREY

Accompanied by a Waltz
Dutch Treat
The Good Fight
Love Comes Silently
Three Fates (anthology)
Work Me Out (anthology)

ART STORIES
Legal Artistry • Artistic Appeal • Artistic Pursuits • Legal Tender

BOTTLED UP STORIES
Bottled Up • Uncorked • The Best Revenge • An Unexpected Vintage

CHILDREN OF BACCHUS STORIES
Children of Bacchus • Thursday's Child • Child of Joy

LOVE MEANS… SERIES
Love Means… No Shame • Love Means… Courage • Love Means… No Boundaries
Love Means… Freedom • Love Means … No Fear
Love Means… Family • Love Means… Renewal

SEVEN DAYS STORIES
Seven Days • Unconditional Love

STORIES FROM THE RANGE
A Shared Range • A Troubled Range • An Unsettled Range • A Foreign Range

TASTE OF LOVE STORIES
A Taste of Love • A Serving of Love • A Helping of Love

Novellas
by ANDREW GREY

A Present in Swaddling Clothes
Shared Revelations

BY FIRE SERIES
Redemption by Fire • Strengthened by Fire

CHILDREN OF BACCHUS STORIES
Spring Reassurance • Winter Love

LOVE MEANS… SERIES
Love Means… Healing • Love Means… Renewal

WORK OUT SERIES
Spot Me • Pump Me Up • Core Training • Crunch Time
Positive Resistance • Personal Training

All published by
DREAMSPINNER PRESS

Readers love Andrew Grey

Dutch Treat

"The emotional pull was strong and the story was great. It was definitely worth reading."

—Long and Short Reviews

A Shared Range

"...another enjoyable read filled with two well-rounded and likable guys."

—Literary Nymphs

Artistic Appeal

"Mr. Grey's amazing storytelling ability captured this reader's attention from the first word and kept me enthralled with the story and the characters within the book until the very last word."

—Night Owl Reviews

The Best Revenge

"...one of the most romantic and heartwarming stories I've read."

—JeffandWill.com

Accompanied by a Waltz

"A story about first love, loss, and the rediscovery of love all wrapped up in its pages."

—Fallen Angel Reviews

http://www.dreamspinnerpress.com

LOVE COMES
Silently

ANDREW GREY

Dreamspinner Press

Published by
Dreamspinner Press
5032 Capital Circle SW
Ste 2, PMB# 279
Tallahassee, FL 32305-7886
USA
http://www.dreamspinnerpress.com/

Love Comes Silently

Cover Art by L.C. Chase
http://www.lcchase.com

ISBN: 978-1-62380-008-6

Printed in the United States of America
First Edition
October 2012

eBook edition available
eBook ISBN: 978-1-62380-009-3

To my partner, Dominic, who, while rarely silent, loves me unconditionally and came into my life at a time when I desperately needed someone to love and love me.

Prologue

KEN moved quietly through the small house, darting around boxes as his insides twisted and turned with every sound that came from Hanna's room. He'd have sworn on a stack of Bibles that he'd unpacked all the bathroom stuff, but he couldn't find the goddamned thermometer. When he'd touched her head, she was hot, and he desperately needed to know how high her fever was. "Daddy," he heard Hanna call weakly, and Ken hurried back up the stairs to her room. Hanna had kicked off her covers and was shivering in her bed, so Ken pulled them back around her, touching her forehead once more before getting a glass of water and a cool cloth that he placed behind her neck as he held the glass for her.

"Is that better, sweetheart?" Ken asked worriedly.

"Yes," she answered as she settled back on the bed, her eyes closing. Ken transferred the cloth to her forehead and then hurried back downstairs. He'd already checked every remaining box upstairs, so he rushed into the small dining room that he was using as unopened box storage and began systematically looking for the missing box.

He finally found it stuck in with the boxes of china that would eventually go in the cabinet that sat empty along the dining room wall. Ken picked up the box, carried it upstairs, and set it on the toilet in the bathroom. He rummaged around inside, not caring what fell on the floor, and finally found the object of his quest. And the fucking thing was dead. He wanted to scream, but began rummaging again until he found the battery charger. He carried everything into Hanna's room, plugged in the thermometer, and let it charge for a minute before placing the tip just inside Hanna's ear. Ken waited impatiently for the soft beep and then lifted it away—103 degrees. That settled it. Ken went to Hanna's dresser and found her tiny robe, placing it on the bed. Hunting around, he found the bunny slippers his parents had gotten her for Christmas the previous year, along with Emily, the doll six-year-old Hanna was rarely without except when she was at school.

"Honey, can you open your eyes for me?" Ken said as he lifted her up. He set her on the edge of the bed as he worked her arms into the robe and got the slippers onto her feet. "I'll be right back," he said and hurried out into the hall, then returned with a blanket. Ken wrapped it around her and then lifted her off the bed, making sure she was covered and warm before leaving the room. He turned out the light with his elbow before descending the stairs.

Ken laid Hanna on the sofa in the half-put-together living room before locating his keys and wallet, coat, and gloves. Then he lifted her into his arms once again. Ken felt Hanna's head rest on his shoulder as he opened the front door.

The frigid air assaulted them both as Ken stepped out into the evening. He closed the door behind him and moved as quickly as he could down the walk to his car. Reaching his keys was another matter, and he couldn't unlock the doors. He didn't have a place to set Hanna down and he could feel her getting cold. By moving Hanna carefully, he managed to pull his keys out of his pocket and click the car doors unlocked. Ken was about to grab for the door when he saw someone reach for the door handle and slowly pull open the back door of his car. Ken glanced at the man quickly before setting Hanna in her booster seat. Ken buckled her in and then closed the door. "Thank you," he said hastily and was able to actually look at the man, who appeared to be about his age, although it was hard to tell under all the winter gear.

The man smiled and nodded, stepping back from the car as Ken opened his door and got inside. The car was ice cold, and he wished he'd have thought to warm it up before bringing Hanna outside. "We'll be warm in a few minutes," he told her as he turned the key in the ignition. Using the wipers to brush away the inch or so of snow, Ken slowly pulled down his driveway and out onto the street. Thankfully, it wasn't snowing right now, and Ken turned on the radio to get the weather forecast as they moved along the plowed street toward the highway. There were very few freeways in Michigan's Upper Peninsula, which had been part of the allure of moving here. One of the things he should have done was choose a house closer to a hospital. Not that he could have expected Hanna to get sick within two weeks of moving into their new home. They reached the highway, and Ken felt heat begin to come out of the vents, so he turned the fan on maximum. After turning onto the recently plowed and nearly clear road, Ken sped up as he drove toward Marquette.

The nerve-racking drive didn't take all that long, not really. It was simply the anxiety of having Hanna sick in the backseat that made the miles seem dozens of times longer than they actually were. Ken had been to Marquette a few times since he and Hanna had moved to Pleasanton a few weeks earlier, and by happy coincidence he happened to have passed by the hospital, so he was actually able to find it. "We're almost there."

"Daddy, I'm thirsty," Hanna said weakly.

"I know. When we get to the hospital, they'll give you whatever you want," Ken promised, his entire being focused on turning into the emergency entrance and then maneuvering the car under the small portico. Ken stopped the car, turned off the engine, and got out. He opened Hanna's door, lifted her out, and then carried her into the emergency entrance and right up to the desk, where a middle-aged woman looked at him with concern.

"She's been sick for a few days and her temperature was 103 when I left the house," Ken began before the woman could ask questions. "I need someone to look at her right away." Ken was feeling frantic. He could feel the heat washing off Hanna and he was afraid her temperature was even higher now than it had been when he'd taken it at home.

"Bring her around to the door," she said as she pointed, and Ken carried Hanna to where the lady had indicated. He heard a buzzing, and then the door opened and a nurse met him and led him through to the emergency treatment area, where he laid Hanna on a bed. He expected to be given a hard time and told to wait, but the nurse began immediately taking Hanna's temperature and vital signs, and then wrote them on a chart as she asked questions.

Ken answered every question. No, she didn't have allergies. She'd been fine a week ago, but she'd gotten a cold that had steadily gotten worse. Ken explained what he'd been giving her and everything he'd done since Hanna had gotten ill. "I'll have the doctor stop by right away," she said and then hurried away.

"Honey, I need to move the car so other people can get help. I won't leave you for very long, I promise," he said, holding her small hand in his. Hanna nodded, and Ken hurried out toward the entrance after telling the receptionist where he was going and that he'd be right back.

Ken flew to the car, parked it, and was back inside in two minutes flat. The doors opened, and he walked to Hanna's bed at the same time as the doctor. "We're going to start an IV to get her rehydrated and see if we can't bring that fever down," he told Ken after looking Hanna over thoroughly. "We're going to run some tests to see exactly what's wrong." The doctor stroked Hanna's hair out of her eyes. "I'll order a bed, and we'll get her into a room as quickly as we can."

Ken nodded as he reached for Hanna's pale hand and held it in his. This little girl, who he'd adopted just two years ago, when Hanna was four, had quickly become the center of Ken's whole world. They'd been looking for a place away from the city where he could raise Hanna in a more rural, down-to-earth setting when he'd found Pleasanton. The town looked ideal, nestled against a small, protected cove on Lake Superior. The views and landscapes were breathtaking, and Ken had been looking forward to painting everything around him. Maybe he would, but first he had to get Hanna better. Little else mattered right now except her.

His phone rang, and when Ken snatched it out of his pocket, he saw it was Mark. He answered in a rush. "I'm at the hospital in Marquette with Hanna," Ken began without preamble.

"What happened?" Mark asked, and Ken heard what sounded like a crowd of people in the background.

"Her temperature spiked and she hasn't been getting better, so I brought her in. They're going to admit her and run some tests." The thought chilled Ken faster than the air outside. She'd been sick for a while and she hadn't been getting better. What if something happened to her and he should have brought her to the hospital sooner?

The noise behind Mark quieted. "She's going to be all right. You did the right thing, and they'll be able to help her," Mark explained logically in his usual reasonable tone. "I stopped for dinner with some friends and I'm heading your way. I have everything packed and I'll be getting on the road in a few minutes. I'll get a hotel tonight and I should be there by early afternoon at the latest."

"Thanks, I'll see you then," Ken said, feeling a bit better knowing Mark was on his way. "I have to go. The doctor just returned. Call me later tonight." Mark agreed, and Ken hung up, shoving the phone back in his pocket. Ken returned to Hanna's side, holding her hand and watching as the nurse spread pain-deadening cream on her arm and put in the port for the IV. Hanna gasped and then began to cry. "I know, honey, but it's almost over and this will help you feel better." He continued holding her hand as the nurse rolled a machine to Hanna's bed and proceeded to attach it to the port.

"You were a very good girl," the nurse said in a level voice before leaving. She returned almost immediately with what looked like a blood kit and began to prepare Hanna's arm. Hanna rolled her head toward him, and Ken saw the fear and confusion in his daughter's eyes. He knew he'd do anything to prevent this. Hell, he'd let them poke *him* with needles for days if it meant Hanna didn't have to endure it. "I'll be gentle, I promise," the nurse said. "I have a daughter about your age, and she has a doll just like yours," the nurse said as she continued working. "What's her name?"

"Emily," Hanna answered, and Ken let go of Hanna's hand so she could cuddle her doll. The nurse inserted the needle and began drawing the blood.

"Did you get her for Christmas?" the nurse asked as she switched vials.

"Daddy got her for me," Hanna explained in her weak voice as the nurse withdrew the needle, putting a Band-Aid with Oscar the Grouch in its place.

14

"That's wonderful. You hold her tight. I know this is a strange place, but as long as Emily and Daddy are with you, there's nothing be afraid of." The nurse stood up, and Ken gave her a smile. "All done," the nurse pronounced and left the room once again, leaving Ken and Hanna alone.

"Close your eyes, honey, and try to rest. They should be in soon to take you up to your room. You won't have to get out of bed or anything," Ken explained, and Hanna held her doll closer with one arm, the other hooked to a machine. Eventually, Hanna closed her eyes and fell asleep. Almost as soon as she did, they arrived to take her to her room. Ken gathered their things and walked alongside the bed; Hanna never opened her eyes.

The room was nice, if sparse, and to Ken's surprise, there was a sofa that the orderly explained folded down into a bed. "Parents often spend the night with their children. I'll be back in a few minutes to make up the bed for you."

"Thanks, I really appreciate that," Ken said before sitting down. He stared at his sleeping daughter, his heart pounding as he thought of all the possible things that could be wrong with her. He hated that she was sick and that Mark wasn't here when he needed him. Ken stood up and walked toward the door, dimming the lights before stepping out into the hall to call the one person he knew would understand.

"Carrie?" Ken said when his call was answered.

"What is it?" his friend asked immediately. She was the person he most regretted leaving behind. "Something's wrong—I can hear it in your voice."

"Hanna's in the hospital. She's been sick and wasn't getting better, and when I took her temperature, it was really high. I'm so worried. She just lies there."

"Is she sleeping?" she asked.

"Yes. They're running tests and won't know anything until tomorrow. They're making arrangements for me to sleep in the room with her." Ken swallowed hard, but the lump stayed firmly lodged where it was.

"It's okay. She probably has a bad case of the flu and the tests will confirm that," Carrie soothed. "Just get some rest and make sure she's comfortable. That's all you can do, and when you hear something, call me right away. I can be there if you need me," she said, and Ken appreciated that, but he knew it wasn't that easy for her to get away from her own family. Talking to her, while helpful and what he needed to hear, only reinforced how alone he felt.

"I'll call as soon as I hear anything," Ken promised, hanging up as the orderly approached. He made up the bed and brought a few blankets and a pillow for him. "Get some rest if you can," he said with an encouraging smile before leaving the room. Somehow, bed or not, Ken knew this was going to be a long night.

KEN woke with a start, wondering where he was. Hanna lay quietly in the bed, and he remembered where they were and why they were here. He stood up, walked to his daughter's bed, and placed his hand on her forehead. At least the fever seemed to be down, and Hanna appeared to be resting comfortably. Opening the door to the room, Ken quietly stepped out and wandered down the dimmed hallway to the nurse's station, where the night shift was working, talking in hushed tones. One of the nurses saw him approach and smiled.

"We have coffee if you'd like some," she told him in a hushed tone.

"Thank you," Ken said. "Hanna's fever seems to be down."

"That's good. I'll be in soon to check on her," the nurse explained, and then she stood up and disappeared into a small room off the desk, then returned with a paper cup. "Here you go."

Ken smiled worriedly and nodded, sipping from the cup. The smooth coffee slid down his throat, soothing him with the familiar in a place that scared him, purely because Hanna had to be there. The nurse went back to work, and Ken wandered back to Hanna's room, leaving the door open slightly for a bit of fresh air before sitting on what he'd used for a bed, sipping the coffee and watching Hanna as she slept. The nurse came in and checked her, and confirmed that Hanna's fever was indeed down before leaving again.

Caffeine or not, after he finished the coffee, Ken must have dozed off again because he awakened when the door to the room opened. "I'm Dr. Helen Pierson, and I've been assigned your daughter as a patient," she said remarkably pleasantly before lightly touching Hanna. "Sweetheart, I'm the doctor and I need to listen to your lungs and heart." Hanna opened her eyes, and Dr. Pierson helped her sit up. She listened to both her chest and back before laying her back down. "Thank you," she told Hanna, who closed her eyes again. "The results of the tests haven't come back yet, but I expect them in the next couple of hours."

"You suspect something," Ken stated, and he could see a flicker in the doctor's eyes.

"We need to wait until we have the test results, and then I'll be happy to discuss anything you'd like. I don't want to speculate at this point. She's resting well, which is excellent, and her fever is definitely down, so that's a good sign. We'll just have to wait a little while longer," she explained. "I'll be by with the results as soon as I have them." She gave Ken a reassuring smile and then left the room.

His phone vibrated in his pocket, and Ken fished it out and walked into the hallway to talk so he wouldn't disturb Hanna. "I

17

just got on the road and I'll cross the Mackinac Bridge in less than an hour," Mark told him.

"I'll be at the hospital in Marquette. When you stop by the house, would you please grab some fresh clothes and my shaving kit for me?" Ken asked, peering into the room because he thought he heard Hanna, but she was still asleep.

Mark didn't answer right away but after a moment he said, "Okay. I'll see you in a few hours." Mark disconnected, and Ken shoved the phone back into his pocket. He didn't have time or the energy for Mark's drama at the moment. He knew Mark hated running errands for anyone, but at the moment, Ken really didn't care. He also knew Mark had a good heart and he'd realize that Ken needed the help about two minutes after hanging up, and then he'd feel guilty.

Ken went back into the room and was greeted by Hanna's blue eyes. She still looked tired, but she was awake. "Are you hungry?" he asked her, and she nodded slightly. "Let me call and get you something to eat," Ken told her before picking up the phone. He talked with the person who answered, and he promised to send up a tray. "You can watch television if you want," Ken told Hanna before turning it on and finding the Disney Channel. Ken didn't normally allow Hanna to watch much television. When they lived in Grand Rapids, they'd spent their time outside, or doing things together. Hanna would draw and color her pictures while Ken painted his. Hanna wasn't his biological daughter, but their interests and talents couldn't have been better aligned. Hanna had the makings of a talented artist; Ken could see it already. She drew beautifully, but she also saw things that other people didn't.

"Can I color?" Hanna asked as she looked away from the television.

"Mark is on the way, and once he gets here, he'll sit with you for a little while and I'll go get your art stuff for you," Ken

18

said. He'd gotten her everything he could think of that was appropriate for her age. Ken settled in the chair next to her bed, and they watched the television together until Hanna's breakfast came. She ate a little and then pushed it aside.

"Aren't you hungry?" Ken asked.

"It's icky," Hanna answered, making the "I'd rather go hungry than eat that" face that Ken knew well. The nurse chose that moment to make an appearance.

"I have some fruit cups, would you like one of those?" she asked, and Hanna nodded. The nurse left and then returned with two small packaged fruit cups. She handed one to Hanna and the other to Ken, who set it aside for later.

"What do you say?" Ken prompted.

"Thank you," Hanna said as she pulled off the cover. The nurse then took Hanna's temperature and vitals before saying good-bye and leaving the room.

Hanna was just finishing the mandarin oranges when the doctor returned. Ken tried to read her face, but he couldn't. "It looks like you're one sick little girl, but we're going to make you better," the doctor said with a smile for Hanna. "Would it be okay if I talked to your daddy for a few minutes? I promise not to keep him too long."

"Okay," Hanna said innocently as she looked at Ken, who pasted as sincere a smile on his face as he could, even though his heart pounded in his chest and his stomach clenched. Ken left the room and followed the doctor down the hall to a small office around the corner. The doctor motioned Ken to a chair and then sat next to him.

"The reason Hanna has been sick is because she has the flu, as you probably suspected," the doctor began. "But the reason she isn't getting better is because we found that she has pediatric leukemia, which has weakened her immune system. We don't know how advanced the disease is at this point. We'll need to run more tests."

The news hit Ken like a sucker punch to the gut. He could barely breathe at all. Closing his eyes, he tried to push away the thoughts that flooded his mind. Never in a million years had he considered that Hanna might have cancer. Ken tried to hold back the tears that threatened to overwhelm him, especially as images of attending Hanna's funeral flashed in his mind.

"Mr. Brighton," the doctor said quietly, and Ken took a deep breath to try to help get his rampant emotions under control. "Take whatever time you need."

Ken reached for a tissue and wiped his running nose. "Where do we go from here?"

"We'll begin with tests and then develop a treatment plan," the doctor explained.

"Should we have her transferred to Ann Arbor?" Ken asked. He was willing to do whatever it took to make sure Hanna had the best care possible.

"You could," the doctor told him. "I don't want to blow my own horn, but you need to know the facts. My family and I moved here from Ann Arbor because my sons wanted to go to Michigan Tech. My husband and I moved with them because we both grew up in the area and because we thought we could do some good for the community. My specialty is oncology, and his is cardiac care." The doctor paused, and Ken blinked a few times, trying to will away the tears, using a tissue to wipe his eyes. "I would be pleased to have Hanna as my patient. I was a senior member of the oncology department in Ann Arbor, and I'm the head of the department here. This little hospital is one of the best in this part of the country. I'm not trying to make your decision for you, though, and I'll support your decision if you want to transfer her."

"Thank you," Ken said with a bit of relief.

"If you stay, she'll also be closer to home, which, when we get to the treatment phase, can make all the difference in the world." The doctor was silent for a few minutes. "Do you have any questions for me right now?" Ken shook his head. He knew he would in the future, but he couldn't think very well right now. "I'm going to go ahead and get the next round of tests ordered. You can let me know what you'd like to do," she said, and Ken nodded. The doctor stood up and left the room quietly.

Ken stayed in the chair, wondering what he was going to do. Hanna had cancer. His precious little girl could die. The doctor hadn't said that, but Ken knew it was true. Ken could almost feel his entire emotional world coming apart at the seams. More than anything right now, he wished Mark were here, just to hear him say that everything would be okay. He needed to hear that even if neither of them knew it was true.

Ken stood, steadying his wobbly legs. Somehow he had to go back to Hanna's room and make believe everything was okay until he got more information from the doctor. Then he could explain to her what was going to happen. For now, she was better off not knowing.

His phone vibrated in his pocket, and he pulled it out and saw the call was from his parents. "Hi, Mom," Ken said, knowing she was the one who always called for both of them.

"How's my precious granddaughter?" she asked, and Ken fell back into the chair.

"Hanna has cancer, Mom," he said, and he heard his mother gasp and then begin to weep softly. Ken placed his head on the desk the doctor had used, unable to hold it in any longer, breaking down into tears as well, and he and his mother shared a long-distance cry.

CHAPTER
One

THE sun shone off everything as Ken walked next to Hanna's wheelchair as the orderly pushed her out of the hospital. Months of treatment that had at times left Hanna almost too weak to lift her head were now behind them. Hanna was showing steady improvement and getting a little bit stronger each day. The air was still cold, so Hanna was bundled up under blankets, but Ken couldn't help hoping that the sunshine that had been so scarce through the winter this close to Lake Superior was a good omen. At the car, Hanna stood up, and Ken rushed around to hold open the door. She was about to get in when the hospital doors slid open and Dr. Pierson walked out in her lab coat, and embraced Hanna. Over the past few months, Hanna had won the hearts of most of the hospital staff, from the doctors to the nurses who brought in special treats so she wouldn't have to eat the hospital food all the time. "You do what your daddy says, and I'll see you in a few weeks," Dr. Pierson said. "And I want another of your special drawings for my office wall."

Hanna smiled. "I promise," she said happily before climbing into the backseat of the car.

"You take care of yourself," Dr. Pierson said as she turned to Ken. "You aren't any good to her if you let yourself get run down. Call me if you have questions or concerns, and if you need help, I'm good at battling with insurance companies." Dr. Pierson smiled, and then, to Ken's surprise, she pulled him into a hug as well. "You're an amazing father and her best chance at a full recovery." She released him and stepped back, waving with the others as Ken got in the car.

"Is your seat belt fastened?" Ken asked, and Hanna belted herself in before turning toward the window to wave at everyone as he put the warm car into gear and slowly pulled away. As helpful and understanding as everyone had been, he was glad to see the hospital disappear in the rearview mirror.

"Daddy, is my hair going to grow back?"

"Yes," Ken said with relief. "You have a few more treatments, and then once they stop and the medicine works out of your body, your hair will start to grow again." When they'd started the treatments, Hanna's hair had begun to fall out pretty quickly. Ken had taken it harder than Hanna had. The doctor had explained it to Hanna and had even given her a pink hat that she'd made from the softest yarn possible. Hanna had thanked her with a hug, and Ken had nearly cried at the thoughtfulness. The doctor had gone on to explain that she had knitted for years and loved making the things for little girls she'd never had the opportunity to do with her two sons. Hanna had worn the hat almost every day since, only taking it off when Ken insisted on washing it.

"Will I be able to go swimming this summer?" Hanna asked as they passed a clearing where they could see Lake Superior, still pretty much iced over.

"I hope so. Lake Superior is probably too cold, but there's a community pool we might be able to use." Ken knew that depended upon the state of Hanna's immune system, which had taken a real beating over the past few months. Hopefully, by then she'd be stronger. "Why don't you ask Dr. Pierson the next time you see her," Ken said, and he saw Hanna nod as she looked out the window.

"Will it be warm soon?" Hanna asked, bare trees passing outside the car.

"Yes. The leaves should start coming out in a few months, and once it gets warm, you and I can go on one of our art walks," Ken told her, and Hanna smiled. Before they'd moved, he and Hanna would spend summer afternoons in the park. Ken would take a sketchbook and Hanna her art set, and they would spend the day drawing and coloring the world around them.

"Will Dr. Pierson come too?" Hanna asked.

"She can if she wants. You can invite her when it gets closer." Ken knew Dr. Pierson was very busy.

"Are you going to marry her?" Hanna asked, and Ken nearly jammed on the brakes in his shock. "I saw you hug her and she hugged you. Does that mean you're going to get married?"

"No. Dr. Pierson is already married and has grown children." There were so many things wrong with that question that Ken didn't quite know where to start. "Where did you get that idea?" Ken asked as he peered quickly into the rearview mirror.

"Callie said once that she came into her mommy and daddy's bedroom and they were hugging, or at least her daddy was hugging her mommy really tight. They told her that hugging is what mommies and daddies do when they love each other," Hanna said happily, as though she understood the mysteries of the universe. Callie definitely knew and saw way too much for her own good.

"Dr. Pierson is my friend just like she's your friend," Ken explained. "Besides, you know I love Mark."

"Because you're gay?" Hanna asked.

"Yes. We've talked about this," Ken reminded her. "I don't fall in love with girls, but I do with boys."

"You love me," Hanna countered.

"Yes. Very much," Ken reassured her.

"But I'm a girl," Hanna countered seriously.

"Yes. You're a girl and I love you. But I'm not going to marry you." Ken had struggled to explain being gay to his daughter, and he'd obviously failed up till now. "Think of it this way. Most men want to marry women and have babies. Instead, I adopted you and I want to marry Mark." Good God, Ken hoped that explained it well enough for her. It seemed to, because Hanna was quiet for a while. Ken knew that could be good, because she was satisfied, or bad, because she was pondering something else.

"What's the difference between boys and girls?" Hanna asked, and Ken found himself pressing down just a little more on the accelerator. This conversation couldn't get over with fast enough.

"What do you think the difference is?" Ken asked, feeling clever that he'd turned the question back on her.

"Boys have penises and girls have 'ginas," Hanna said, and Ken breathed a sigh of relief. "Girls also get boobs, but some men do too. Daddy, will you get boobs?"

Ken laughed. "No. Not if I can help it?"

"Will I get boobs?" Hanna asked.

"Yes," Ken answered, starting to laugh. If Hanna asked one more question about boobs, penises, or vaginas, Ken was going to run screaming from the car. "How about we see who can be quietest the longest. I'll bet you ice cream I can beat you."

Hanna opened her mouth to argue with him, but then she slapped her hands over her mouth, and Ken could see she was smiling. The rest of the trip was quiet, and ten minutes later, Ken pulled up in front of the house. "You win. After dinner, you can have ice cream," Ken said, and Hanna laughed as Ken turned off the car before getting out. He opened the door for Hanna, and she unhooked her seat belt before climbing out of the car.

Ken got out as well, popping the trunk so he could grab their bags before following her up the walk. It had been months since Hanna had been home, and Ken doubted she really remembered their house.

Hanna was halfway up the walk when a gust of wind, cold and straight off the lake, blew across the yard. Hanna shivered at the cold and hurried toward the house. She'd just reached the steps when her hat blew off her head, the air lifting it for a few seconds before carrying it across the lawn. "Daddy," Hanna cried, and Ken hurried to where Hanna stood. He set down the bags and hurried after it, but didn't reach it before the wind picked the hat up again, blowing it across the street, and Hanna's favorite pink hat ended up in a mud puddle. Hanna began to cry, and Ken hurried to her, lifting her into his arms.

"I'll get it, and once it's washed it'll be as good as new, I promise," Ken said as he carried her into the house out of the wind. He set her on the sofa and heard Mark walking through the house. Hanna was still upset as Mark came in the room. "Would you stay with her for a minute?" Ken asked and then hurried back outside.

As he descended the steps, Ken saw his neighbor walking toward him, carrying the sodden hat with an almost sorrowful look on his face. He didn't speak as he handed over the once pink hat, now brown, with twigs stuck to it. He'd obviously wrung it out, but he didn't say anything.

"Thank you," Ken said. "My daughter just got home from the hospital and this is her favorite hat." Ken waited for him to say something, but the man didn't. Instead, his eyes conveyed that he felt badly for Hanna. "She has to wear hats all the time because she lost her hair." Why Ken was telling him this he didn't know, but the man looked as though he was hanging on every word.

"Daddy," Hanna called from the door.

"I have to go," Ken explained. "Thank you so much," Ken said, and the man smiled and waved before turning to walk back down the sidewalk. Ken watched him leave for a few seconds, sort of getting lost in the way he moved. Then he realized what he was doing and hurried back toward the house, hoping Mark hadn't seen him watching someone else.

"Is it okay?" Hanna asked as Ken approached.

"It will be, honey. Go on inside. I'll bring the things in and wash it right away for you," Ken explained, and he stopped to pick up the bags. Hanna disappeared into the house, and Ken couldn't stop himself from looking to where his neighbor had gone. He saw him standing a few houses down watching him. He waved, and Ken did his best to wave back before walking into the house.

"I need to talk to you," Mark said almost as soon as he'd closed the front door.

"Okay," Ken said. "But I have to get Hanna settled in her room and then do some laundry." He held up the sodden hat. "We can talk once I get her to sleep." Ken moved away and hurried to get to work. Getting Hanna settled was the most important thing right now.

Ken got Hanna situated on the sofa under a blanket and let her watch television as he hurried through the house trying to get things done. He unpacked the things they'd brought home from the hospital, made Hanna something to eat and drink, and took them in to her before descending the stairs to the basement so he could get the laundry started. He had a lot to do, but he was still happy. Hanna was home with him once again and hopefully on the mend.

In the laundry area, Ken sorted the dirty clothes and got the washer started. "You haven't hummed in quite a while," Mark said from behind him. Ken finished loading the clothes before closing the lid on the washing machine.

When Ken turned around, he didn't see the happy, open expression he expected. Rather, Mark's features were pinched, he had bags under his eyes, and Ken even noticed a few wrinkles that hadn't been there a few weeks ago. They'd both been through a lot in the past few months, and Ken moved closer, ready to pull Mark into his arms, but Mark took a small step backward, and Ken stiffened. "We need to talk," Mark told him, and Ken sighed, nodding slightly.

"I'll meet you in my studio in a few minutes," Ken said, and Mark nodded before walking away. Ken heard his footsteps on the stairs as he finished up with the laundry. Once he was done, Ken climbed the stairs, turning off the lights before checking on Hanna. She was quietly watching television, resting under a pink blanket. She looked a little pale, but still as precious as ever. Looking away from the television, she smiled at him, and Ken walked over to the sofa, kissing her on the forehead.

"Are you okay, Daddy?" Hanna asked.

"I'm fine. I'll be out in my studio if you need anything," Ken said, and Hanna nodded, returning her attention to the television. Before leaving the room, Ken picked up Hanna's art case from the hall and placed it near the sofa. She'd been watching a lot of television in the hospital, and Ken was hoping to entice her back to the things she'd always loved before she'd gotten sick. "Don't forget the picture for Dr. Pierson," Ken told her softly.

"I won't," Hanna answered, and Ken left the room, walking down the hall and out to the small room that had been added onto the house by the previous owner.

Mark sat on the old sofa the movers had placed against the one wall, a sofa Ken had never moved. There were still boxes that had never been unpacked and canvasses leaning along the other wall. Ken hadn't painted in months; his heart and mind hadn't been in it. He'd been fully occupied with Hanna.

"Sit down, Ken," Mark said as he stood up, and Ken sat on the edge of the sofa. "I'm not quite sure how to say what I need to say," Mark began as he wandered slowly through the room. "Things aren't working between us anymore. They haven't in a while," Mark said, and Ken stared at him as he moved. "You've been taking care of Hanna, I know that, and you needed to. I don't begrudge her your attention. But even before she got sick, things weren't particularly good between us. We slept together and lived in the same house, but we're moving in different directions." Mark's voice trailed off, but he continued pacing the room.

Ken opened his mouth to deny what Mark was saying, but he couldn't, not really. He'd been living at the hospital almost constantly for months, and though he'd called Mark every day, in two months they hadn't talked about anything other than Hanna and how she was doing.

"You know I'm right, and I'm not doing this to hurt you," Mark continued.

"I know," Ken finally managed to say. "You never did anything hurtful the entire time I've known you." Ken sighed, wondering if there was anything he could say. "Why did you move with us, then?"

Mark stopped pacing and sat down next to Ken on the sofa. "I honestly thought that things might change between us once we moved. We would be working together to set up our new home, making new friends together. I really thought building a new life in a new place would bring us closer, like we were right after you got Hanna, but it hasn't worked, and I don't think it will. Circumstances got in the way, and I don't think our relationship is reparable. Do you?"

Ken thought about it for a long time and then shook his head. "You're probably right," he whispered. Ken had honestly thought Mark was the man he'd spend the rest of his life with. Ken had been in the early stages of adopting Hanna when he met Mark, and he'd been supportive and loving through the ups and downs of the entire process.

"Don't get me wrong. I love both you and Hanna and I always will. But I've been giving this a lot of thought over the past few months, and to be honest, we probably would have had this conversation a while ago if it hadn't been for Hanna getting cancer. I couldn't have this talk with you then, and I'm trying to not be a dick about things."

"What are you going to do?" Ken asked, feeling both hurt and a bit relieved. The more he thought about it, the more he realized that Mark was probably right. It was time they got on with their lives, and while that would have once meant working through everything together, now it meant going their separate ways.

Mark humphed softly. "Kenny, we've drifted apart to the point where you haven't even noticed that most of my things are already gone. I have an apartment in town, and I'll move the last of my things out later today."

"Is there someone else?" Ken asked, and Mark shook his head.

"I'd never do that to you or Hanna, you know that," he answered with a touch of hurt in his voice, and Ken nodded.

"I do know that. You're a good man, you always were," Ken began. "I'm going to miss you, and so is Hanna."

"I'm going to miss you too. I'll still be in town, and we can still see each other and talk. I want us to be friends, and I still care about both you and Hanna. I just think it's time we look at things logically and make a break of it before we come to resent and hate each other, and we will. You need all your efforts concentrated on your work and Hanna. I need to start building my own life." Ken felt Mark's hand slide into his. "I do love you, Kenny, I probably always will, but this is for the best. I think we'll both realize it pretty quickly." Mark let go of his hand and walked toward the studio door. "I'm going to load the last of my things into the car and say good-bye to Hanna. Maybe in a few weeks, we can all have dinner together or something."

"Okay," Ken answered, standing up himself.

"You'll see that I'm right," Mark whispered before leaving the room. Ken stayed where he was, glancing around the empty studio, waiting for the hurt and rejection to hit, but they didn't. At times like this, he'd normally feel the need to paint, but that didn't materialize either. Ken closed the door behind him as he left the studio, walking through the house until he heard Mark softly talking to Hanna. Leaving them alone, Ken went into the kitchen to start something for their dinner, but he didn't really feel like doing anything at all. Eventually, he heard footsteps and knew Mark was getting the last of his things. Ken joined Hanna in the living room. The television was off and she had a pad resting on her legs as she colored, her tongue sticking out slightly between her lips as she concentrated.

"What are you doing?" Ken asked, sitting next to her on the edge of the sofa. He half expected to be bombarded with questions, but Hanna kept working.

"I'm drawing a picture for Mark," she explained without looking up, and Ken watched her for a second. She didn't ask him anything, so Ken stood up and sat in one of the nearby chairs. Mark came into the house and walked down the hall and up the stairs, returning a few minutes later with his suitcase.

"I'll call you in a few weeks," Mark promised as he headed for the door. After setting down the suitcases, Mark walked over to Hanna, saying good-bye to her before kissing her forehead.

"This is for you," Hanna said, handing Mark the drawing. "So you don't forget Daddy and me."

Ken blinked away the tears that threatened as Mark thanked Hanna. "I could never forget you, munchkin." Hanna threw her arms around Mark's neck, giving him a hug. "Things didn't work out between your daddy and me, but that doesn't mean either of us love you any less." Then Mark stepped away and looked at him. Ken took a deep breath and gave Mark a hug.

"Take care of yourself," Ken whispered before releasing Mark and watching his lover and partner of almost three years leave the house for the last time. Ken closed the door behind Mark and then walked back into the living room. He refused to allow himself to do anything as maudlin as watch his car drive away for the last time.

"Daddy, does this mean Mark isn't your boyfriend anymore?" Hanna asked, her eyes widening.

"Yes. That's exactly what it means," Ken explained with a sigh. Mark was probably right. They had been drifting apart for a while, but that didn't mean he didn't feel the loss or the loneliness. He might not have been with Mark while he was spending those long hours at the hospital, but that didn't mean he hadn't missed him or wasn't comforted simply by the fact that Mark was there. Now he and Hanna were alone, and he wasn't sure how he felt about that. Maybe he wouldn't know for quite a while.

"I'm gonna miss him, Daddy," Hanna said softly, her lips quivering slightly.

"I know you will sweetheart. So will I. But you still have me, and you'll always have me, no matter what," Ken said as he tried to hug away the fear he saw in her eyes.

"Promise?" Hanna asked,

"Yes, I promise," Ken said. He and Mark wanted different things from life, and while Mark hadn't necessarily picked the best time to leave, him hanging around for Hanna's sake was only going to make Mark unhappier and wasn't going to help Hanna's recovery, which was the most important thing. "I'll never leave you, ever."

Hanna remained quiet for a long time and then moved out of Ken's embrace. "Will you get another boyfriend?"

"Maybe someday," Ken said with a slight snort, wondering just how much boyfriend material there was in a town like Pleasanton. Marquette had to have a gay community of some type, but that was most likely dominated by college students. "Right now, I'm going to work on helping you get well," Ken said, changing the subject. "I'm going to try to figure out something for dinner. Why don't you draw me a picture?"

"I will if you will," Hanna said, and Ken smiled.

"How about if I turn on the heat in my studio? You could move in there, and I could start putting things away." Ken needed to keep busy. Over the past two months, he and Mark had unpacked most of the house a little at a time. Maybe it was time he unpacked his studio and considered getting on with life. He needed to try to get some semblance of normality back for both of them. "Let me get the room warmed up, and then you can sit at one of the easels if you want." That got him a grin, something Ken hadn't seen as much as he liked over the past few months, and seeing that expression again was worth all the worry and exhaustion he'd been through.

Ken had left the room and was walking back through the house when the doorbell rang. Ken pulled the door open and saw their neighbor standing on the stoop holding a casserole dish. He simply smiled and extended his hands, covered by oven mitts. "Thank you," Ken said and motioned for him to come inside. His neighbor looked around and then took a tentative step inside. Ken closed the door. "That smells wonderful."

"Daddy, is that macaroni and cheese?" Hanna called, and Ken heard her scurrying toward him, the blanket wrapped around her shoulders. "Ooooh, my favorite," she said as she smiled up at their neighbor, and Ken saw him grin at Hanna, a gorgeous smile that extended all the way up to his eyes.

"The kitchen's this way," Ken said, wondering why their neighbor was being so nice and why he was so quiet. He obviously wasn't shy, or he would have stayed away. "That smells wonderful," Ken commented appreciatively as he placed the dish on one of the stove burners. "Would you like to join us for dinner?" Ken asked, but their neighbor shook his head and quietly headed for the door. Ken followed and opened it for him. "Thank you so much, again," Ken said and watched in near total confusion as the man hurried away down the walk and then along the sidewalk toward his house.

"Are you hungry?" Ken asked Hanna after closing the door.

"I guess," she answered, but Ken found her standing near the dish of macaroni and cheese. He got her a small plate as well as one for himself, and they sat together at the table eating a sumptuous feast. After they'd both eaten way too much, Ken turned on the heat in the studio before cleaning up the dishes.

Then he and Hanna moved into the warm room. Ken set her up with an easel, and then he began unpacking mobile metal racks and then his painting supplies, putting everything away in the exact spot he wanted it. When he was working, Ken often lost himself in his art, searching for supplies by feel more than sight when he got engrossed in his work.

By the time Ken had unpacked everything, he considered trying to work, but Hanna was tiring, and he didn't want her overdoing it, so he made sure everything was where he wanted it before quietly stepping to where she was working. "What are you making?"

"It's a picture of you, Daddy," Hanna said before lifting the drawing to show it to him. It really did look like him. The hair color was right—light brown with a touch of blond here and there. She had reproduced his blue eyes and even the slight crookedness to his nose from where he'd broken it as a kid. Her eye for detail was pretty amazing for someone so young, and being able to transfer that to the paper was even more impressive.

"It's wonderful," Ken told her. "Let's pack up and we can get you a little something else to eat before bed."

"Mac-cheese?" she asked, and Ken smiled as he nodded.

Hanna gathered her things, and Ken put a small bowl of the macaroni and cheese in the microwave for her, careful not to get it too hot. When she joined him in the kitchen, Ken got her settled in her booster chair at the table, and she ate while he puttered. Ken wasn't hungry, so he kept busy, and once Hanna was done, he shooed her upstairs for a bath.

It took Ken longer than normal to get Hanna bathed and into her pajamas. He had to be careful of the port near her shoulder that they used for her treatments, and he couldn't help treating her with kid gloves. She was all he had, and he'd almost lost her, or at least that was how he felt. Mark was gone, so it was just him and Hanna now. "Let's get you into bed, and I'll read you any story you like."

"*Madeline?*" Hanna asked as she scurried into her room. By the time Ken wiped up the bathroom and came into her room, Hanna was already under her covers, grinning up at him excitedly as he found the book and began to read. Ken barely made it halfway through the story before Hanna's eyes began to close, and by the time he finished, she was sound asleep. He made sure she had her doll before turning off the light and flipping on the tiny butterfly nightlight on the far side of the room. After partially closing the door behind him, Ken finished cleaning up the bathroom before getting ready for bed himself. He'd spent months taking care of Hanna in the hospital, and now, when the house was quiet, he was at loose ends, and he wished he had Mark to talk to. Before Hanna had gotten sick, they would sit up and simply talk, for hours sometimes, about anything and everything. At least that was how it had been once, but that was a while ago. Ken sat on the edge of the bed, looking over at the side where Mark had always slept. Even his pillow was gone.

Ken blamed himself. He'd taken Mark for granted. He'd loved Mark, but he'd also expected him to be there when he needed him. Maybe if he'd paid more attention to him…. He knew it was his fault, and that Hanna's illness was just the straw that had broken the camel's back. Mark hadn't left because of Hanna; Ken never thought that for a second. Mark loved his daughter. Mark had left because of him—that was the only explanation. Mark was gone, and whether Ken was right about why or not, that didn't change anything at all. Ken turned out the light and slid under the covers, staring up at the ceiling, playing "what if" recrimination games with himself until he finally fell asleep sometime in the wee hours of the morning.

His bed rocked and Ken cracked his eyes open, knowing that Hanna had crawled into bed with him. "I heard a noise downstairs," she told him as she climbed under the covers on the other side of the bed. "Maybe it's a bear."

"It's probably the man delivering the paper," Ken told her before closing his eyes once again. Hanna seemed to accept the answer, and Ken drifted back to sleep listening to the soft sound of his daughter's breathing.

Later, Ken felt Hanna get out of the bed. Peering through slitted eyes, Ken looked at the clock before groaning and then getting out of bed. The house felt cold, and he could hear the wind whistling around the corners, making the room feel colder than it was. "Let's get dressed, and I'll make you some breakfast," Ken told Hanna, and she returned to her room. "Do you need me to help you?"

"I'm not a baby!" Hanna cried back, and Ken smiled as he quickly dressed and cleaned up before going to see what kind of mischief Hanna had gotten into. He got a pleasant surprise when Hanna joined him outside her room dressed in clothes that matched, and she hadn't managed to pull all the clothes out of her dresser to find them. She was carrying her shoes, though, and Ken scooped her into his arms, laughing as he flew her down the stairs, both of them making airplane noises.

They played all the way into the kitchen. Then Ken set Hanna down and began making breakfast. "You can get the newspaper," Ken told Hanna, and she hurried to the front door. The words were on the tip of his tongue to have her walk and take it easy, but seeing her with energy, even if it only lasted a few hours, was very heartening.

"Daddy!" he heard Hanna squeal, and he stopped what he was doing so he could take a look at what had her so excited.

The front door stood open, and Hanna was outside in the wind, peering into what appeared to be a box. "What is it?" Ken asked as Hanna lifted the box and brought it inside before closing the front door with a slam.

"Hats," Hanna said delightedly, and she began pawing through the box, lifting out hat after hat. There were some of every style imaginable: knit caps, wide-brimmed frilly hats, an old-fashioned stocking cap that dangled down Hanna's back. There was even a small pillbox hat that made Hanna look adorably retro. "Where did they come from?" Hanna asked him without stopping to look up from her bounty.

"Was there a note?" Ken asked as he looked through the box, but he saw only the hats.

Ken's phone rang, and he fished it out of his pocket, surprised to see Mark's number. "Hello," he said tentatively.

"How are you?" Mark asked. "I just called to make sure you were okay." The sadness in Mark's voice was clear even over the phone. "Is that Hanna I hear?" She'd chosen that moment to squeal with glee when she saw a puffy pink hat. She placed it on her head before dancing around the living room. "She sounds happy," Mark said.

"I think she is," Ken agreed with a smile. "That was very—" He was about to thank him for the hats.

"Ken, I have to go," Mark said in a rush, and Ken thought he heard Mark's voice crack slightly. "I only called to make sure you and Hanna were okay. I was out running some errands this morning and I'm frozen to the bone. I'll call you later... soon." The call ended, and Ken stared at the phone for a few seconds before setting it on the hall table. Ken wondered at the strange phone call and figured it was Mark's way of making sure they'd found what he'd left for Hanna.

"Let's get some breakfast, and then you can try on each of the hats," Ken told her before lifting Hanna into his arms and carrying her to the kitchen.

CHAPTER
Two

PATRICK FLAHERTY had seen the little bald girl's reaction to the box of hats he'd placed outside the front door of the house she shared with her father. Patrick had found out the man with the beatific smile and eyes so deep it looked like the worries of the entire world would fit inside them was named Ken, and that he was some sort of artist. He hadn't heard much else about him, other than he was new in town and that his daughter had been very sick. Patrick did know from watching him that the other man who'd lived in the house had been Ken's boyfriend, but he appeared to have moved out, and now it was just Ken and his daughter. That was fine with Patrick. He'd noticed the other man the very first day he'd moved in two houses down the street from the small house Patrick had inherited from his mother. Not that he had any illusions that Ken had noticed him, other than to see him outside working.

People in town had been talking about Ken and his daughter for months, their tongues flapping like a flag in the wind off Lake Superior. Apparently, Ken Brighton was some really famous artist, with his paintings hanging in museums and selling for big bucks all over the country. That was one thing Patrick had found out very quickly after the accident that left him nearly completely silent—people figured that since he couldn't talk, he couldn't hear, either, or think. Patrick clenched the handle of the snow shovel as his anger and hurt welled inside. He was the same person he'd been before the accident, and he wished he could make others see that.

After watching the front of the house for a few seconds more, Patrick let the squeal of joy he'd heard drifting on the wind bring a smile to his face as he returned to his chores. He had to get these done before the snow that had begun to melt hardened into ice he'd never get off the sidewalk.

Patrick worked for nearly an hour, and he was about to put his shovel away when he saw Ken and his daughter come out of the house. He couldn't suppress a grin when he saw the little girl was wearing the poofy pink hat he'd given her. She held her father's hand, and Patrick walked closer, waving at both of them. He saw the little girl wave back at him before she pulled her hand from her dad's and walked down the sidewalk toward him.

"Hello," she said with a smile. "Thank you for the mac-cheese, it was really good." Patrick nodded and smiled, watching as the girl cocked her head curiously. Patrick touched his throat and shook his head. "Can't you talk?" she asked, and he shook his head.

"Hanna, don't bother the nice man," Ken said as he came up behind his daughter.

"Daddy, he can't talk," Hanna said to him. Patrick was used to the pitying looks or even tsking sounds when people found out, but Ken smiled at him and extended his hand.

"I'm Ken Brighton, and this is Hanna," he said as he firmly shook Patrick's hand. Once Patrick let go, Patrick pointed to the embroidered name on his coat. One thing he'd begun doing after the accident was have his name added to his jackets and coats. It was the best way he could figure out to easily tell people his name. "It's nice to meet you, Patrick," Ken said with an ease that Patrick rarely saw in others. Most people didn't quite know how to react to him. "We both wanted to thank you for the macaroni and cheese. It was fabulous," Ken said, and Patrick began to shift slightly under the other man's piercingly perceptive gaze.

Patrick smiled once again and nodded, placing his hand over his heart in a gesture that meant their thanks was appreciated.

"We're going to the store, and then Daddy and I are going to paint," Hanna told him excitedly.

"We need to get going," Ken said. "You shouldn't be out in the cold for very long." Ken might have been talking to Hanna, but he continued looking at him, almost studying him. "Thanks again for the food. I'll return the dish later today," Ken added with a slight smile, and Patrick felt his insides jump a little. Patrick waved as the two of them walked back to the car, and after getting inside, Patrick saw Hanna wave as they drove away.

He'd been attracted to Ken since the first time he saw him. But he quickly found out that he had a boyfriend, so Patrick did what he usually did—pushed his interest aside and went on with life. Granted, he wasn't sure if the boyfriend was really gone, and if the relationship had just ended, then his handsome neighbor probably wasn't looking for someone else right away. Not that he'd be particularly interested in Patrick, but he could dream. He watched until the deep green car disappeared from sight before putting his shovel away in the garage and then opening the door to the attached workshop.

Patrick turned on the lights, looking over his woodworking shop and the chest of drawers that he'd been working on. He made his living making fine handcrafted furniture, and he had an order he had to get completed, so he put the way his neighbor moved beneath his clothes and the depth of Ken's eyes out of his mind and got to work.

THE hours Patrick spent in his workshop were regularly some of the most enjoyable of his day. He got to take an ordinary piece of wood, and with work and love, turn it into something beautiful.

"Patrick," he heard from behind him, and he turned off the planer as his cousin Julianne stepped into the workshop. "I called for you four times," she said, and Patrick shrugged. There wasn't much he could do. He didn't have a phone out here and he didn't want the interruptions, either. "You haven't been in the diner this week, and I was worried about you." If he didn't show his face every now and then, the mother hen would come looking for him.

Patrick lifted his hands and showed her that he had all his fingers before turning around so she could see he was in one piece and hadn't wasted away to nothing.

"How anyone can not be able to talk and still be such a smartass is beyond me," she chided, slapping him on the shoulder. "But you manage it in the first ten seconds." Julianne was the only real family Patrick had left, and he loved her dearly. She checked up on him and had him over for dinner with her family from time to time. "So you're alive. Is there anything new?"

Patrick rolled his eyes, and Julianne placed her hands on her hips and waited. Patrick began to slowly pantomime what he wanted to say. He and Julianne had developed a sort of sign/body language of their own. It had slowly developed over the years since his accident. She'd often said that she'd take classes with him to help him learn to sign, but Patrick kept putting it off. He didn't want to learn because it sort of meant giving up hope. "Your neighbor's daughter came home from the hospital?" Julianne said tentatively, once Patrick had finished. "That's really nice. Is she okay?"

Patrick nodded with a smile, smoothing his hand over his head.

"Oh, she lost her hair," Julianne said. "So that's why you bought all the hats yesterday." There were definitely no secrets in this town. Everyone knew everything about absolutely everyone. At least that had the side benefit of letting him talk less. Julianne set her purse on the workbench and pulled up a stool, settling in for a while. "Did she like them?" she asked, and Patrick nodded, pantomiming her reaction, to both his and Julianne's delight. "Do they know they were from you?"

Patrick shook his head, his expression turning serious. That he'd made Hanna and her dad happy was all that mattered, and seeing them out together with her wearing one of the hats he'd given her was all the reward he needed.

"You don't want them to know, do you?" Patrick shook his head again. "Why?" Julianne asked as she stood up and walked around the bench. "You have the kindest heart of anyone I've ever met, and not everyone is going to reject you because you can't talk." Patrick scowled and knitted his brows at Julianne. He knew the expression was exaggerated, but that was part of how he communicated. "I doubt they're those kind of people," Julianne added, and Patrick relaxed his expression. She was probably right, in fact more than likely right, but still….

Patrick looked around the workshop and found a piece of paper. "*I took mac and cheese like Mom used to make and Hanna really liked it. She said thank you and was wearing one of the hats I gave her*." Patrick passed the note to Julianne who read it and nodded. Patrick took the paper back. "*She seems like a very sweet little girl*," he wrote.

Julianne smiled at him. "Sounds like she's a real cutie."

Patrick colored, and Julianne got one of those knowing looks that always made Patrick squirm. When they were kids, he could never get away with anything around her because she could figure him out in two seconds. Now, she seemed even more in tune with him, and he turned to one of his machines.

"Turning away isn't going to do you a bit of good," Julianne teased. "I saw the way you blushed." He heard the stool skid on the floor and then her footsteps as she walked toward him. "You know, it's okay to like whoever you want." She touched his arm. "It's her father that's really caught your interest, isn't it?" Patrick nodded, but didn't turn around. "You know I loved your folks to pieces, but about you being gay, my aunt and uncle were full of shit!" Julianne told him with a touch of venom in her voice. "They filled your head with that nonsense to the point that you believe it, but they were wrong. And if they were still alive, I'd tell them so and you know it. So stop listening to what they filled your head with and follow your heart. You deserve to be happy just like anyone else."

Patrick reached for the pad of paper, trying to think how he could explain it to her, but he couldn't. Even if he had his voice, he wasn't sure he could tell her, and writing it down was damned near impossible. "*It doesn't matter. He just broke up with his boyfriend,*" Patrick wrote.

Julianne read it and then laughed. "Yes, he may need some time to heal, but that doesn't mean you should sit on the sidelines and wait until the time is right." Julianne went quiet, and Patrick knew she was up to something. "If you're not sure, then it wouldn't hurt to become his friend. We could all use more friends."

Patrick touched his throat, and Julianne chuckled before giving him a hug. "Sometimes words are overrated," she quipped. "You'll figure out a way." Julianne moved toward the door, her long coat swaying as she walked. "Stop by for dinner on Sunday," she commanded, and Patrick saluted her as she pulled open the door. "Stop being a pain in my ass or I'll serve brussels sprouts," she threatened, and Patrick made a face.

After Julianne left, Patrick didn't feel like going back to work, so he cleaned up, left the workshop, and went back to the house. It had begun snowing again, but he wasn't in the mood to shovel again, either, so he went inside and began making dinner. Patrick loved to cook, but he didn't like making dinner for just himself. There was something lonely about it, and he always ended up making too much and then eating the same thing for the next week. He went ahead and made dinner anyway, then sat down at the same table he'd eaten at since he was a kid. As he began to eat, he thought about what Julianne had said. Patrick had accepted that he was gay for some time now, but he'd only done something about it once before, and that had been, well, nice to start with, but... he hated to even think about it. He'd never told his parents, because they would never understand. Then there was the accident, and....

Patrick sighed and ate a bite of pasta, looking around the room. Maybe Julianne was right. Looking at the kitchen, Patrick knew he hadn't moved on. It looked the same as when his mother was alive, as did most of the rest of the house. How could he ever expect to move on with his life if he was still living in the past? Or worse, someone else's past? He had to do something about that. Patrick glanced around the room once again, this time with a critical eye. He needed to paint and take down all the cutesy decorations his mother had always collected. Maybe he could make himself a dining table and chairs. He'd made enough of them for other people. Patrick finished his dinner as he thought of all the things he'd like to do with the house.

As he was cleaning up, his doorbell rang, and Patrick walked through the house to answer it. He couldn't remember the last time someone other than Mormons or canvassers had knocked on his door, and they'd been a bit disappointed when he wouldn't answer their questions. There were times when not being able to speak was a blessing. He opened the door and was surprised to see Hanna standing on his doorstep, with her father behind her.

"Daddy and I baked cookies," Hanna said, and Patrick smiled at the plate of oddly shaped cookies. Obviously Hanna had helped quite a bit.

"They taste better than they look," Ken said, and Patrick took the plate with a smile before motioning them inside. It had been quite a while since he'd had company. He half expected Hanna and Ken to decline, but Hanna stepped inside and walked into Patrick's living room. He turned on lights and then set the cookies on the table before going to the kitchen for glasses of milk. He wondered what they wanted as he opened the refrigerator to pull out the carton of milk he'd gotten that morning. Peering in the refrigerator, he wondered if he should offer Ken a beer. He didn't really drink very often, but he pulled two of those out as well. If Ken accepted one, he wouldn't let him drink alone. After putting glasses, the milk, and the beer bottles on a tray, he carefully walked back into the living room, wondering how awkward this visit was going to be.

"I made you a picture," Hanna said as Patrick set the tray down on the coffee table. The little girl didn't seem in the least shy, and when he sat down, she sat next to him. Patrick watched as she then jumped back up and rummaged in the pocket of the coat she'd placed in one of the chairs. As she did, Patrick noticed with a smile that she was still wearing the pink hat he'd given her. It pleased him that she liked it. Hanna found what she was looking for and returned to the sofa, bouncing down next to him. Patrick wasn't used to people he'd hardly met being comfortable with him. Hell, there were days when he wasn't comfortable with himself. "This is to thank you for the mac-cheese. It was really good," Hanna explained with the tone and smile only a pleased little girl could muster. It must have been the same tone they used to wrap their fathers around their little fingers. She handed him the paper, and Patrick unfolded it.

His eyes widened. He had been expecting the crude, barely discernible drawing of a little girl. He hadn't expected a picture of himself that actually looked like him. Patrick opened his mouth out of an old, nearly forgotten habit and began to say "thank you," but of course no sound came out. He wanted to scream in frustration that he couldn't make a sound and never would again. Oh, he could grunt and make sounds like an animal, but not the sounds of a human being, not like he used to.

"You're welcome," Hanna said, and Patrick looked at Ken for an explanation, hoping she wasn't making fun of him. He'd had people make fun of him before and he ignored it, but he knew this little girl doing it would hurt.

"Hanna is very intuitive," Ken explained, his expression clearly shining with pride in his daughter.

"Is it true you can't talk?" Hanna asked innocently before going on without waiting for an answer. "Because Daddy says I sometimes talk enough for two people, so maybe I'm talking for you too." Hanna reached for a cookie, and Patrick tried to keep the dumbfounded look off his face. Patrick pulled open the coffee table drawer and took out a pad and paper. He thought writing things down might help, but then he realized Hanna wasn't likely to be able to read yet. Instead, Patrick wrote the note and handed it to Ken. Their hands touched for a split second as he passed it over, and Patrick wished he could touch Ken again, but that was way too forward. "What does it say, Daddy?"

"Patrick said that he was in an accident and he was hurt and lost his voice," Ken read from the note in his rich, resonant voice. "Do you know sign language?" Ken asked, and Patrick shook his head. "Was the accident long ago?" Patrick raised two fingers to indicate about two years ago. After picking up a bottle of beer, he raised it to Ken, who smiled. "Thank you."

Patrick poured Hanna a glass of milk, and she thanked him as she took it, then reached for another cookie. Patrick saw her looking around the house and he chuckled roughly—at least the accident hadn't taken that bit of sound from him. "*The house was my parents', and I haven't had a chance to do much with it,*" he wrote and then handed the paper to Ken, who nodded.

"I understand. Sometimes there are more important things," Ken told him as he looked at Hanna. Patrick had kept his heart closed for a long time. Probably too long, like Julianne sometimes said, and he could feel the first stirrings, maybe the first chink in the walls he'd built up over the years. Anyone who loved his daughter as much as Ken obviously did was someone he'd give almost anything to have love him. He nearly scoffed at the thought and forced his attention back to his guests. Hanna snagged a cookie and then took another one and handed it to him. Patrick ate it, making a show of how much he liked it before taking another. "What do you do?" Ken asked, and Patrick pointed to the coffee table, then ran his hand over the smooth finish. "Did you make that?" Ken asked, and Patrick smiled, nodding proudly. "How long have you been doing that?"

Patrick spread his hands apart to indicate a long time. He'd been making things with wood since his father first let him tinker in his woodshop. Patrick reached for the paper and wrote again, looking up from time to time at Ken's patient expression. "*But I've been making my living crafting furniture for two years,*" Patrick wrote, and he saw Ken read the note and watched as understanding shone on his face. He could almost see the next question lining up in Ken's mind, and Patrick braced himself for the disappointment that always accompanied the story of what he'd lost, but Ken didn't ask, to Patrick's relief.

"Thank you so very much for the mac-cheese. It was one of the most thoughtful things anyone has done in a while," Ken said. "Bringing Hanna home has been wonderful and hectic." Ken looked like he wanted to draw his daughter into his arms and hug her forever.

"*Is she going to be okay?*" Patrick wrote.

"Yes. She has a few more treatments, and then we wait to make sure everything we've done has been successful." The hope and love in Ken's eyes for his daughter filled Patrick with longing to have someone care for him that way. "That's the really hard part for both of us," Ken added.

Patrick turned, watching as Hanna set her cookie on her plate. "Then my hair will start to grow back," Hanna informed Patrick brightly, and he smiled and nodded. Patrick wanted to hug her and say that she was lucky, and that like her daddy said, everything would be all right. She was so innocent and open, and he wished like anything that Hanna's father was right and that what he hoped came true. Patrick knew it didn't always work out, because everything hadn't been all right for him. So often people told him he was lucky, and in some ways, he knew he was. If the injury had been just a little off, he probably would have died, but instead he'd been left without the ability to talk. There were worse things, he supposed, but even now, there were times when he was hard-pressed to think of them.

Hanna munched on her cookie once again, and Patrick watched as Ken did the same. The room was quiet except for the sound of chewing and glasses being set on the coasters. Situations like this were often uncomfortable for Patrick, but as he ate his cookie, he kept seeing Hanna and then Ken smiling at him like they understood that, sometimes, silence was golden.

"Did you ever learn to talk with your hands? I had a friend before we moved here who talked with her hands because she couldn't hear. She learned me how to say some things," Hanna told him happily before setting down her cookie and jumping to her feet to stand across the table from him. She proudly made some signs. "That means sky," Hanna informed him, and Patrick nodded. "And that means house," Hanna said before sitting down once again.

"Hanna, finish your cookie. It's getting close to your bedtime, and you can't overdo it if you want to get better," Ken prodded lightly, and she nodded, nibbling on her cookie like a large mouse. Patrick knew she was eating more slowly on purpose, and from the indulgent expression on Ken's face, he did as well. Patrick watched a smile split Ken's face, and Patrick smiled as well, as loneliness unlike anything he could remember welled up inside him. This was a man he could love. He knew it was dumb to think that, but he knew it could happen just from the love Ken showed his sick little girl. For a few seconds, he let hope expand inside him as he thought that maybe someone with as big a heart as Ken seemed to have might come to love him. "Come on, honey, finish your cookies and milk. You'll see Patrick again."

Hanna did as she was told, eating the last of her cookie and then finishing her milk before she picked up her coat. Ken helped her put it on along with her mittens. "Bye, Mr. Patrick," Hanna said, and as he leaned down to say good-bye to her, she put her arms around his neck and hugged him. Patrick lightly hugged her back before letting go.

Ken extended his hand and Patrick shook it. "Thank you," Ken said, and Patrick nodded, knowing Ken understood. Ken put on his coat as well before lifting Hanna into his arms. Patrick opened the door, watching as they left the house and headed down the walk back toward their own home. Patrick lifted his hand in a silent wave. Both Hanna and Ken waved back, and then Patrick stepped inside and closed the door.

He cleaned up the few dishes from the living room before wrapping the cookies and placing them on the counter. He shut off the kitchen lights and then sat in the family room and turned on the television to while away the time before he was ready to go to bed. As he flipped through the channels, he caught a glimpse of an old rerun. The remote slipped out of his hand and bounced on the floor, and the batteries rolled under the sofa. He tried looking for the batteries, but they were out of reach. He could hear the television show continuing behind him. "And now a new and one of the brightest stars to come along in a very long time," the announcer said. Patrick lunged for the television, slapping the button to turn it off. The silence reverberated through the room, almost deafening in its complete lack of sound.

Patrick sat in a heap on the floor, staring at the dark screen for a long time just to make sure it didn't come on again. Then, after gathering the batteries from under the sofa, he slowly stood up. After putting the remote back together and somehow restraining himself from throwing it through the television, he set the controller on the table beside his chair and turned out the lights before climbing the stairs to go to bed. There were times when he wanted to sleep his entire life away. There was no pain, no longing, and in his dreams, he was free to be who he'd always wanted and what he'd wished for since he'd been a child was his once more. In his dreams, he could be whole again.

CHAPTER
Three

THE sun shone, creating a world of almost blinding whiteness everywhere. "Daddy, can I go outside?" Hanna asked as she jumped on his bed in a burst of energy that made Ken smile. "Look, Daddy, my hair is longer now," Hanna told him with a grin. She had obviously just come from the bathroom to tell him, like she had each morning for the past week. Her light blonde hair was just a fraction of an inch long, but Ken couldn't help placing his hand on her head to feel the downy hair. It was another sign of Hanna's recovery and gave hope to both of them.

"It's still a bit too cold. I know it's sunny and it looks warm, but it isn't."

"But Mr. Patrick is outside," Hanna told him with sad eyes, and Ken felt the last of his resistance fail him. Hanna loved their silent neighbor, and Ken couldn't stop himself from parting the curtain on the window near his bed to look out. Patrick was indeed outside, clearing the sidewalks of the slush before it could refreeze. The tall, silent man fascinated him, and Ken had found himself watching him every chance he got.

Patrick was handsome, there was no doubt about that, and something about him drew Ken's eye no matter what. Even now, watching him as he worked, Ken could see his almost fluid grace as he moved. There hadn't been many times that Ken had seen his neighbor without his thick coat and all bundled up against the weather, but when he had, he hadn't easily been able to keep his eyes to himself. Patrick was strong, there was no doubt about that, and as Ken peered out the window, he saw Patrick bend down to fill his shovel. Ken closed his eyes and swallowed hard as his mind conjured up Patrick's pants tightening around his butt and thick legs.

"Daddy," Hanna said with a slight whine that she was probably entitled to after Ken's mind had wandered off six ways to Sunday.

"Okay. We'll bundle you up tight and you can spend a little time outside, but you have to take it easy. Remember what the doctor said the last time you saw her," he warned, and Hanna nodded.

"I know, Daddy," Hanna agreed, and Ken felt a stab of guilt the way he always did when he tried to stop Hanna from doing things children her age normally did without thought.

"Go back to your room and pick out what you want to wear," Ken told her, and Hanna climbed down off the bed.

"I already did," she said with a smile and hurried away. Ken pushed back the covers and got out of the bed. After tugging off his pajamas, he pulled on clean underwear and then jeans and a shirt before hurrying to the bathroom. He knew he had about five minutes before Hanna came looking for him again.

Right on time, she banged on the bathroom door as he was brushing his teeth. Ken spit out the toothpaste and rinsed his mouth before opening the door and then lifting Hanna up so she could do the same. "Wash your face and hands, and then you can get dressed and eat."

"Daddy, I wanna see Mr. Patrick before he goes inside," she whined, and Ken nodded.

"Then you'd better hurry," he told her, and she washed and dried her hands and face before rushing back to her bedroom. The doctors had all told him he'd know as soon as Hanna was truly feeling better, and that certainly seemed to be the case right now. She had energy that Ken hadn't seen in a while. By the time he caught up with her, she had already stripped off her nightgown and was pulling on her little underwear.

"Those are backward, honey," Ken explained, and he helped her get them on before picking up the pants and shirt she'd chosen. He helped without appearing to help too much, and once she had her socks and shoes on, they both went downstairs. Hanna started pulling on her coat and then handed Ken her mittens so he could help her get them on properly.

Once Hanna was bundled up, Ken got his gear on and then opened the front door. They stepped outside, and Ken made sure she got safely down the steps before she took off down the walk toward where Patrick was working. Ken watched as the big man set down his shovel to greet Hanna with a hug. "Morning, Patrick," Ken said, waiting for Patrick's smile and a gentle nod. He'd come to learn a lot of things about Patrick, not least of which was the fact that he had what seemed like a million different smiles, and each one said something different. This one said, "I'm happy to see you." "Hanna saw you from inside and insisted we come out to visit. I hope we aren't interrupting your work," Ken said, and Patrick's expression shifted to one of delight and he rolled his eyes slightly.

"The doctor says I'm doing very well, but I have to take it easy," Hanna explained with one of her own patented eye rolls that Ken swore she'd picked up from Patrick. Sometimes he thought those two had developed their own language; maybe they had. He knew there were things about Patrick that he picked up that Hanna hadn't, like the way his eyes shone or the way Patrick looked away whenever Ken caught him watching. So why wouldn't Patrick and Hanna have also developed their own signals? Over the past few months, Patrick had developed into one of Hanna's favorite people, and she always seemed to know where he was and what he was doing. It was sometimes spooky.

Patrick lifted Hanna into his arms, and she giggled and laughed as he held her high so she could look out over everything. After a few moments, he set Hanna down, and Ken watched as Patrick showed her how to make a snowball. He formed the snow in his hands and then lobbed it through the air where it blew apart against the side of a tree. Hanna mimicked his movements and threw the snowball at Ken, who tried to jump out of the way.

"So you want to snowball fight," Ken said, and Hanna squealed her delight as she scooped up more snow and threw it at Ken. The air soon filled with loose snowballs, bits of snow, and laughter, some of the latter coming from Patrick. Ken felt his heart skip a beat when he heard the rough sound. At first Patrick choked off the sound, but when both Ken and Hanna continued their laughter, Patrick seemed to let go a little, laughing in his own way. Ken caught a bunch of snow in the face when he was paying more attention to Patrick, and the way his face lit up when he smiled, than he was to defending himself against Patrick and Hanna's combined assault.

Ken grabbed a pile of snow and began flinging it at both of them, most of it raining down in flurries long before it reached its intended target. Ken found himself laughing as he let go of the worry that had plagued him for months. "Take that!" Ken cried and lobbed a loosely packed snowball at Hanna. It hit her foot, and she squealed and laughed as both she and Patrick retaliated in a thick wall of snow that left him covered from head to toe.

Everything stopped when Hanna coughed. Ken had to keep himself from rushing to her. She didn't do it again, but Ken looked at Patrick, the concern that their fun had momentarily pushed aside rushing back. Hanna continued to play until Patrick touched her shoulder. She looked up at him, and Ken swore they had some sort of meeting of the minds, because Hanna stopped and then coughed again. Ken was ready to take her inside when Hanna removed her elbow from in front of her mouth, the way she'd been taught. "Daddy's making pancakes." She looked at Ken with an impish grin. "Right, Daddy?"

"Whatever you want," Ken told her, lifting Hanna into his arms.

"Daddy makes the bestest pancakes there are," Hanna told Patrick before turning in Ken's arms. "Can Mr. Patrick have pancakes too?" she asked, and Ken knew exactly what the little scamp was doing. Hanna was only six, but that girl knew how to wrap any man in her life around her little finger, especially when she looked at them with her big blue doe eyes. No one could say no to that face as she peered out from under her pink fuzzy hat.

"Patrick is always welcome to have pancakes," Ken said. "Please join us." Patrick motioned up and down the sidewalk, indicating that he had a lot of work to do, and Hanna pouted, as if on cue. Ken could see Patrick's resolve crumble like a snow fort in July. "I'll have breakfast ready in about half an hour. Please stop by if you like." Ken knew it wouldn't be right to pressure Patrick, so he gave him an out. Hanna waved good-bye, and Ken carried her back toward the house as she coughed again.

Inside, Ken got her coat off and sat her down on the sofa. "You need to take it easy." Ken turned on the television and let Hanna watch some cartoon that made no sense to him, but Hanna was engrossed and quiet. In the kitchen, he got out the ingredients for pancake batter and began mixing it up. He hoped Patrick would join them, but he wasn't counting on it. Their silent neighbor always seemed reticent in any social situation, but Ken enjoyed his company. Patrick fascinated him. He wasn't sure why, and he sometimes wondered if it was the fact that he was silent and distant, sort of unattainable.

Ken listened as he worked, and thankfully he didn't hear Hanna coughing any longer. He'd finished the batter and was about to begin heating the griddle when the doorbell rang. "I'll get it, Daddy," Hanna called, and Ken was about to stop her when he heard her pad to the front door. The resounding squeal told Ken it was indeed Patrick, and he came into the kitchen with Hanna in his arms.

"You need to rest—you know that," Ken told Hanna, and she pouted for a second before turning to Patrick.

"Can I watch a video?" Hanna asked. Ken was about to set down the batter and help her when Patrick motioned that he'd do it, and the two of them left the kitchen. "I want to watch *Barbie Nutcracker*," Hanna said. Ken heard the television go silent, and a minute later the now familiar music from the start of the video began.

Ken poured the first pancakes on the griddle as Patrick came back into the room. "She loves that," Ken told Patrick as he worked. "A few weeks ago, I got up to get the paper and a box of children's videos was sitting on our front porch." Ken set the batter aside and watched the pancakes cook. It was either that or stare into Patrick's eyes, wondering at the pain behind them, or at his lips and wonder just what they would taste like. "I don't know who's doing it, but I suspect it's my ex-boyfriend, Mark. He's called every now and then, and it's always after something has been left for Hanna." Ken made sure the pancakes weren't sticking as he watched Patrick. He'd also thought Patrick might have left the box, but there was no reaction whatsoever. "She loves the Barbie *Nutcracker* video. Hanna's watched it almost daily." The familiar music continued playing in the other room, and Ken turned the pancakes. Then he reached up into the cupboard and pulled down a plate that he set into the oven before turning it on warm.

Once the pancakes were done, Ken placed them on the plate and returned them to the warm oven before putting a new batch on the griddle. Ken motioned Patrick to one of the stools before getting out orange juice and milk from the refrigerator and then setting them on the table. "Hanna loves my pancakes," Ken explained. "And I think it's because they're about the only thing I can cook that doesn't end up burned or raw." Patrick smiled, and Ken got out flatware and set the table before turning the pancakes. "Hanna, come in to the table," Ken called, and he heard the video pause; then Hanna walked in and took her place at the table, motioning for Patrick to sit beside her. Ken got the pancakes out of the warm oven and set the plate on a cloth on the table.

"Please help yourself," Ken told Patrick as he poured juice and milk. Patrick helped Hanna with her pancake before taking a few for himself. Once Ken had everything set, he filled his plate. Before he could eat, Ken made sure Hanna had butter and just the right amount of syrup on her breakfast before fixing his own. Ken watched as Hanna began eating. She always ate slowly, and Ken had developed the habit of watching how much she ate. When she'd been so sick, she'd eaten very little, and it was good to see her actually eating the way a normal child would. He also saw Patrick practically wolf down his pancakes. Either the man was hungry or the breakfast was actually pretty good. Ken began to eat as well, and he realized a few things: the pancakes really were just average, and the smile that seemed to brighten Patrick's face just might be for him.

"Daddy, can I have more juice?" Hanna asked, and Ken poured her another small glass before feeling her forehead. He seemed to do that all the time, though Hanna felt cool and normal.

Patrick reached for another helping of pancakes. "You really don't have to eat them to be nice," Ken told Patrick, and he shook his head, giving Ken another of those eye rolls before eating once again. There were so many things he wanted to ask Patrick. The man was gorgeous and intelligent as hell, but so closed off. "Did you ever look into one of those computers that helps you talk? Like Steven Hawking has?" Patrick set his fork on the plate with a rattle, and Ken wondered if he'd done something wrong, but Patrick didn't seem angry as much as sad. "I'm sorry. I didn't mean to…."

Patrick shook his head and touched Ken's hand. Without thinking, Ken turned his hand over and felt Patrick's fingers lightly scrape over his. Ken couldn't take his eyes off where Patrick was touching him. His rough skin moved slowly over Ken's. Finally lifting his gaze, Ken caught Patrick's, and they stared at each other until Hanna began to laugh.

"Daddy and Patrick, sitting in a tree…." Hanna sang in her clear little girl voice. Ken smiled and glanced at her, but when he looked back at Patrick, the sadness was back, and much deeper this time. Hanna continued to sing, and Patrick gently pulled his hand away.

"Shhh, honey," Ken whispered, and Hanna stopped singing and looked alternately at Patrick and then Ken, clearly as confused by Patrick's reaction as he was. Hanna's lower lip began to quiver, and Ken placed his hand on her shoulder, quelling the anger that threatened to bloom inside him. "It's okay," he said softly to Hanna, and she sniffled. Patrick stood up quickly, his chair nearly overturning as he stepped back from the table.

"I'm sorry, Patrick," Hanna said as she looked up at the stricken expression on Patrick's face. He stood without moving for a few seconds and then seemed to realize all of a sudden how he'd acted. "I was just playing," Hanna said, and Patrick's expression softened. The knot that had formed in Ken's stomach unwound just a little. He had no idea what had caused Patrick's distress, and he hoped it wasn't what he'd asked him, but it seemed to be dissipating, and some of the stress and tension flowed away. Ken motioned toward the chair, and Patrick slowly sat down once again and took Hanna's hand in his, an apology written in Patrick's expressive eyes.

Ken saw Hanna smile, and then she returned to her breakfast. Ken tried to return to his, but kept watching Patrick, who took a few bites and then set down his fork again. Ken stopped eating as well and watched as Patrick looked around the table. Ken opened the drawer behind him and found a small pad and pen, which he handed to Patrick. After a few seconds, Patrick handed the pad back to Ken. "*I didn't want to sound like a computer,*" Ken read before lifting his gaze to Patrick and nodding slowly. Patrick took the pad back, and Ken took a bite of pancake, chewed, and swallowed while Patrick wrote, not taking his eyes off him the entire time. Eventually Patrick handed him the papers after tearing them off the pad, and Ken read what Patrick had written, a chill running up his back as he did.

"*I used to be a singer,*" Patrick had written. "*All my life that was all I ever wanted to do. I sang all the time since I was nine years old.*" Ken looked up from the paper and saw Patrick writing some more. Lowering his gaze, he checked on Hanna before continuing to read. "*All I ever wanted to do was sing. I thought about going into opera, but I met a man when I was in college. He'd heard me sing at a small club on campus and asked me if I'd be willing to sing for him.*" Ken set down the papers, and Patrick handed him more. "*That man was Devon Rand. He helped me make my first record and then my second. He also arranged for me to go on tour. He was like family.*" Ken could barely continue reading the words, his heart ached so hard for Patrick. He could almost feel the loss. Without thinking, Ken reached over to Hanna, placing his hand on her shoulder. He needed to feel her because the fear he'd had of losing her was the only thing that came close to how Patrick must have felt. *"Two years ago, I was in Chicago after a performance. We were celebrating a new record deal as well as a sellout concert when a man entered the restaurant and started shooting. I got hit in the throat."* The words on the paper ended, and Ken looked up to see that Patrick had pushed his plate aside and had his head down on the table with what looked like two additional pieces of paper clutched between his fingers.

"It's okay, Patrick," Hanna said as she slid down off her chair and walked over to where Patrick sat. She tapped his shoulder, and when he sat back up, Hanna climbed onto his lap and hugged him. Ken saw Patrick look over her shoulder, then push two small pieces of paper toward him.

"The doctors said it was a miracle I wasn't killed." Patrick's writing was getting hard to read, but that might have been a combination of what Patrick was feeling and Ken's watery eyes. *"There happened to be a doctor in the restaurant and he managed to keep me from bleeding to death. He helped me breathe, and when help arrived, he went with me to the hospital. I can barely remember much of it, but I remember waking up on a hospital bed with tubes down my throat."* Ken placed the pages on the table, unable to read any more. He had a pretty good idea of what they said anyway.

"Hanna," Ken said as he lifted her off Patrick's lap and set her on her feet. "Please go into the living room and watch your video, I need to talk to Patrick, okay?" She nodded and slowly left the room. Ken carried her juice into the living room and got Hanna settled before returning to where Patrick sat at the table. After sitting down next to him, Ken lightly touched Patrick on the shoulder. "I'm sorry about what happened. Was it Hanna's singing that…?"

Patrick shook his head before taking a deep breath and pointing toward the papers. Ken picked them up again and began to read, wondering just what Patrick wanted to say. "*I couldn't talk or swallow and I could barely keep my eyes open. There was a hole in my throat with a tube that I was using to breathe.*" Ken read as fast as he could. "*The doctors all said I was lucky to be alive, and then they gave me the bad news that I would never talk again. At first, I didn't believe them, but over the weeks as I began to heal and the tubes came out, when I tried to speak, all that came out were grunts and noises. My throat hurt all the time, and I kept thinking that the doctors were wrong and that over time I would talk again. But I never did.*" Ken set down the paper and read the last sheet. "*Eventually I came back here and tried to build some sort of life for myself away from the stage and the life I'd known and wanted.*"

Ken set the last page on the table, looking at Patrick as he stared back. "I don't know what to say." Patrick shrugged and pointed to the bottom of the page where Ken saw the name Pat Flaherty printed cleanly, and he gasped. Ken knew that name. In fact, he had both the albums Patrick had referred to earlier in his notes. Ken stared at Patrick, almost unable to believe what he'd been reading. But he also seemed to remember Pat Flaherty suddenly disappearing, and at the time Ken had wondered why. Now he knew. "I loved your music, but that wasn't everything you were then or are now." Ken stood up, touching Patrick on the shoulder. "I'm sorry about what happened to you, and I can understand why you'd rather be silent than sound like a computer." Ken leaned forward, put his arms around Patrick's neck and pulled him into a hug that felt so right it nearly took Ken's breath away. "I know what it's like to lose, or in my case, nearly lose something very precious." He felt Patrick nod against his shoulder and heard a soft sound. He wondered if Patrick was trying to speak, but the sound ended and Ken felt Patrick's arms wind around his waist.

"Daddy," Hanna called from the other room, and Ken released Patrick from the hug.

"I have to see what she wants," Ken explained, and Patrick nodded. As Ken walked toward the other room, he wondered just how many people knew Patrick's story, and he realized there couldn't be many that he'd ever taken the time or the effort to explain to just what had happened. People in town must know who he was and the barest outline of events, but Ken figured he was in exclusive company to have Patrick explain what had happened in his own words. "What is it, honey?" Ken asked as he approached where Hanna sat watching television.

"Is Patrick going to be okay?" Hanna asked as she looked up at him.

"Yes. He was just upset, but it wasn't anything you did," Ken explained, and he heard footsteps. Turning around, he saw Patrick standing in the doorway with his coat on, nodding his thanks. "You're welcome anytime," Ken said, hoping Patrick would visit again.

Hanna slid off the sofa, hurrying to where Patrick stood. "I'm sorry if I made you sad. I won't pick on you anymore." Patrick lifted her into his arms, and she hugged him enthusiastically. "I promise," she said before adding, "even if you decide to kiss Daddy." She added that last part in her version of a stage whisper before bursting into a fit of giggles. Patrick smiled as well before setting Hanna down, and Ken saw him to the door, part of him wishing Patrick would take Hanna up on her offer and kiss him. He wanted to kiss Patrick and hold him in his arms, but he wasn't sure either would be welcome, so he opened the door. "Thank you for joining us and for telling me your story." Ken touched Patrick's shoulder as he passed. "I know you don't explain that to many people, and I appreciate the courage and trust it took to tell me." Patrick nodded and half smiled before walking out the door.

Ken closed the door and leaned against it, thinking. "Daddy, can I have some more juice?" Hanna asked from the other room, and he hurried in, scooping her up off the sofa to giggly protests.

"Yes. I'll bring you juice, and you can work with me in the studio," Ken said, and he carried Hanna to the kitchen, grabbing a plastic cup and the juice along the way. Hanna was still giggling as he set her down in front of where she'd been doing her drawings. They hadn't been in the studio in quite a while. Ken turned on the heat, listening to the registers ting softly as they heated up. Hanna settled and began to draw as the room warmed, and Ken began opening the drawers behind him, pulling out tubes of paint after he'd set a canvas on his easel. The white canvas was already gone, colors and shapes already filling his vision. The rest of the world around him faded to the background, and Ken felt the usual tingle as the vision of what he wanted to do came into focus. That hadn't happened in such a long time that he barely recognized the feeling as his heart raced and the blood pounded through his veins. Reaching for a brush, he began to apply paint directly to the canvas.

Often with his ideas, he sketched and worked out his thoughts thoroughly before actually placing it on the canvas, but the feeling was so strong and the image so clear, he simply began to work.

Ken lost all track of time as he continued working. The only person outside of himself that he was aware of was Hanna, and she worked quietly at her table, drawing and coloring. After a while, she said she was hungry, and Ken got her something to eat, remaining in a bit of a fog until he got back to his canvas. Eventually, Hanna curled up on the old sofa, and Ken covered her with a blanket and kissed her on the forehead before returning to work. He continued working, and it wasn't until he heard Hanna stirring that he cleaned out his brushes and put everything away. Sometimes, when he worked this way, he worked as fast as he could because he was always afraid his vision would fade, but this one was so strong and rich that he knew he'd remember it for months. When he had everything cleaned up, Ken glanced at the clock, surprised that he'd been working for most of the day. "Come on, sweetheart. I'll make you some dinner, and we can watch television together."

Ken took Hanna's hand and led her to the kitchen, where he made a simple dinner that he somehow managed not to burn, and then he settled with Hanna on the sofa. Together they watched one of the DVDs until it was time for Hanna to go to bed. Ken helped her get ready and then tucked her in. "What story would you like?"

"*Madeline*," Hanna said excitedly, and Ken began to wonder just how many times he was going to have to read her this story before Hanna had it memorized, but he grabbed the book and sat on the edge of her bed before opening the book and starting to read. Tonight he made it all the way through the story with Hanna wide awake. Ken turned out the light and then kissed her good night.

"Sleep tight, and I'll see you in the morning." Ken kissed her on the forehead again. "I love you, sweetheart."

"I love you too, Daddy," Hanna said as she rolled over, cuddling her doll, and Ken quietly left the room, closing the door partway before he walked back to the living room. Ken flopped down in his chair and turned on the television. After ten minutes, he still had no idea what he was watching—some show about icebergs or something. In the silence, he sat, and the image for the painting began to play in his head. Ken got out of the chair, walked to his studio, and grabbed a brush and paints.

He didn't do anything as dramatic as close his eyes; he didn't need to. The image he wanted was right in front of him. He'd been seeing it in his mind for hours. Patrick's eyes already stared out at him for the canvas, and he was about to start work when he rushed back inside, then returned with two CDs that he placed in the player. Beautiful music began to play, and then the richest, deepest voice Ken had ever heard began to sing, and he felt tears come to his eyes knowing that voice was gone forever. Without thinking, Ken picked up his brush and got to work.

For hours, he worked on the nose and cheeks, getting just the right shade and coloration. Then he moved to the throat to get the muscles just right, and the chin lifted ever so slightly. Once he had that, he moved to the mouth, and then stopped, his brush paused just above the canvas as the music ceased and the room fell quiet. The spell broken, Ken stood without moving for a few moments, almost afraid to place his brush on the canvas. He thought of starting the music again, but he didn't want to do that. Slowly, he set his brush down and stepped away from the easel, staring at the unfinished work. He still had hours of work to complete it, but he was amazed by what he'd gotten done so far. After cleaning everything up, Ken left the studio, turning off the lights after himself, and headed upstairs.

Ken checked on Hanna before heading to the bathroom to clean up and get ready for bed. He turned out the light and climbed beneath the crisp, cool sheets, shivering a few times before his skin warmed. Staring up at the ceiling, he willed the unsettled feeling away, but it wouldn't leave. Part of him wanted to jump back out of bed and go to work again, but Ken knew he couldn't force it. His mind needed time to process what he was feeling and what he was really striving to get onto that canvas. Closing his eyes, he rolled onto his side and tried to calm the pictures that continually flashed in his head. It was funny, but he hadn't been in the mood to paint at all for months, since Hanna's diagnosis and Mark's departure, but now he couldn't stop image after image from flooding his mind. Eventually, Ken got out of bed and pulled on a pair of sweatpants and a sweatshirt before hurrying back to the studio. He set aside the painting he'd been working on, put another canvas on the easel, and went to work, this time on a huge canvas that would be life-sized. He knew exactly what he wanted to paint, but he had to start on the face.

Ken worked for hours before eventually curling up on the sofa with the blanket Hanna had used pulled up over him, and he didn't wake until he felt Hanna shake him. "Daddy, I'm really hot," Hanna said, and Ken flew off the sofa like he'd been shot.

Ken's heart skipped a beat as he touched Hanna's forehead. She had a slight fever, and he lifted his daughter into his arms and carried her back through the house to the sofa, where he laid her down and then covered her with a blanket. "I'll be right back," he told her before getting a glass of juice. After he returned, Ken set down the glass and turned on the television for her. Once she was settled, Ken went back to the kitchen and called the doctor. Thankfully, he was put right through. He told Dr. Pierson that Hanna had a slight fever, but she didn't seem too concerned.

"There's a lot of bugs going around right now. Make sure she rests and gets plenty of fluids. If the fever doesn't go away in the next day or so, I want to see her," she said, and Ken heard the doctor rustling some papers. "Scratch that. I have an opening this afternoon. Bring her in, and we'll have a quick look. It's most likely nothing, but I want to be sure. Hanna's been through a lot. Have you got any Tylenol?"

"Yes," Ken answered, doing a quick mental check.

"Give her one and see if it brings down the fever, and I'll see you this afternoon." The doctor's confidence calmed his nerves, and Ken thanked the doctor before hanging up. Ken made a light breakfast with cinnamon toast for Hanna and got the Tylenol before carrying in a small tray. Hanna looked tired, but alert, as he set down the tray.

"Dr. Pierson thinks you have a slight cold," he told Hanna as he touched her forehead. She seemed cooler already, and Ken thought he might have turned the heat up a little high and she overheated with all the covers on her bed. "We're going to see her this afternoon."

"Are they going to poke me?" Hanna asked, drawing her arms under the covers.

"They might," Ken answered as he sat on the edge of the sofa. "But you've always been such a big girl." Ken handed her the plate of toast after he got her comfortably sitting up. "I've always been so proud of you." Ken felt his emotions coming to the surface. "In the hospital, you never complained." Ken took the plate from Hanna and set it on the coffee table before pulling her into a gentle hug. "I love you more than anything in the world."

"I love you too, Daddy," Hanna said. "Can I eat now?"

Ken chuckled and released Hanna, giving her back the plate before standing up and pushing the table closer so she could reach her cup of juice. "Do you need anything else?"

"No, Daddy," Hanna answered, already engrossed in whatever show she was watching. Ken glanced around the house as his worry lessened and the need to work through what he was feeling came to the front.

"I'll be in my studio if you need me," Ken said, and Hanna nodded as she picked up a piece of toast and took a bite.

Ken didn't work the way he usually did, because he would not allow his mind to sink into the painting as he worked. He had Hanna to worry about, and every half hour or so, he'd go in to check on her. About lunchtime, she said she was hungry, and when Ken touched her forehead, her fever seemed to be gone. He verified it with the thermometer and breathed a sigh of relief. He made her some chicken nuggets and then went back to work for a few hours before cleaning up and getting Hanna ready to visit the doctor.

HANNA hugged Dr. Pierson when she opened the examination room door. "You seem to be doing much better," Dr. Pierson said as she lifted Hanna onto the table. "Let's take a look and make sure it's just a touch of a cold." Ken fidgeted nervously as Dr. Pierson looked in Hanna's throat and ears, then listened to her heart and lungs. "Your throat is a bit red. Does it hurt?" Hanna nodded, and Dr. Pierson threw the wooden stick away before taking off her gloves. "As we thought, it's just a cold. I'm going to give you some medication to help with the symptoms," the doctor told Ken. "Her immune system is still a bit weak, so make sure Hanna gets lots of fluids and keep an eye on her breathing and temperature the way you have been."

Ken nodded. "Thank you," he said with a small sigh of relief.

"I'm going to ask the nurse to take some blood, and we'll run some tests while you're here so you won't have to come in next week," Dr. Pierson told Hanna, and she nodded, biting her lower lip. "You can ask the nurse for a lollipop on your way out if you're good." Ken rolled his eyes, and Hanna nodded with a slight smile. "I need to talk to your daddy for a few minutes."

Ken followed the doctor outside and they closed the door. "She's doing very well, and you did the right thing. A full-on cold or the flu could really knock her down at this stage."

"I thought I was overreacting," Ken admitted, but the doctor shook her head.

"You did just fine. I want to keep a close eye on her." The doctor patted Ken's shoulder reassuringly. "Take good care of her and she'll be fine." The doctor smiled warmly before heading down the hall. Ken went back inside and sat with Hanna until the nurse came to draw blood. Hanna gasped a little when the nurse poked her, but otherwise she sat still until it was over, and the nurse gave her a sucker.

"Am I done?" Hanna asked.

"All done," the nurse told her, and Ken took her down off the table. After gathering their things, they walked toward the front desk. Ken took care of the prescription and instructions for Hanna, and soon they were on their way.

Ken stopped at McDonald's to get Hanna a treat, and they sat in a corner booth away from the other patrons while she ate her chicken nuggets. Ken's phone rang, and he noticed it was Mark.

"Kenny, I stopped by the house and no one was home." He always seemed to get right down to business now. It still hurt some that the calls that once made his heart race simply from hearing Mark's voice had now become clinical and almost businesslike.

"I had to take Hanna to the doctor. She has a cold, but they wanted to check her out," Ken explained, and Hanna grinned from across the table. "What did you need?"

"Nothing in particular," Mark said rather softly. "I was missing you and I thought maybe we could talk. There's no reason we shouldn't be friends, and I was curious how Hanna was doing."

"We're both fine, and we should be friends. We were together for two years," Ken said as he shuffled the phone so he could help Hanna squirt the ketchup out of the little packets. "I guess I'm a bit surprised, that's all. If you'd like to come by some day next week, we could have lunch and talk." Ken didn't know why he was offering, but it seemed like the nice thing to do. "Hanna would like to see you too."

Mark hesitated before agreeing. "Should I bring anything?" Mark asked, and Ken chuckled. "Okay, I'll bring the lunch when

I come," Mark said, adding his own laughter. "I sometimes wonder how you two keep from starving on your own."

Hanna stood up and leaned over the table. "Daddy takes me to McDonalds," she said into the phone, and Ken heard Mark laugh once again.

"I thought it was something like that. Okay, I'll call you next week and we can set something up." Mark disconnected, and Ken shoved his phone back into his jacket pocket.

"Mark is going to come visit next week for lunch," Ken told Hanna, and she shrugged before taking a bite of one of her nuggets.

"Can Mr. Patrick come too?" Hanna asked with her mouth full, and Ken glared at her for a few seconds. Hanna placed her hand over her mouth and then took a drink of her juice as she swallowed. "Please, Daddy." It was plainly obvious who Hanna's favorite person was at the moment.

"I don't think Patrick and Mark would get along," Ken explained, and Hanna accepted the answer, or at least seemed to as she began eating again. Ken highly doubted Patrick would be willing to come to lunch with Mark there. "Finish your food so we can get you home. You need to rest." Hanna began eating more slowly, and Ken started clearing away the trash. "You can sit in my studio with me and draw if you want."

Hanna shook her head. "It's stinky in there now," she told him before grabbing her nose.

"Okay. You can watch television and draw if you want," Ken placated, and she finished eating. After Ken cleaned up, he helped Hanna into her coat and carried her through the slushy parking lot. Once he got Hanna settled in her seat, Ken started the car and turned the heat on high as he maneuvered through the already darkening afternoon along the now very familiar road between Marquette and Pleasanton.

After pulling up to the house, Ken stopped the car and unlocked the doors. Hanna got out of her seat and then out her door, rushing quickly up the walk. "Hanna, wait," Ken called, but she didn't stop until she reached what looked like a large shoebox next to the door.

"Daddy!" She practically screamed as she tore open the top of the box. Ken followed up the walk in time to see Hanna pull out what looked like a Barbie doll. "Look at these," she cried happily.

"Let's take it inside," Ken said, looking around. Just like the other boxes, there was no note or card, but Ken knew Mark had been by the house, so he was convinced that he'd left the box for Hanna, and reminded himself that when Mark came to lunch the next week, he'd thank him. He would have to stop at a bakery to get the cheesecake that Mark loved. It was the least he could do. Ken picked up the box and unlocked the house before ushering Hanna in out of the cold. He set the box aside and got Hanna's coat and mittens off before settling her on the sofa under a blanket with her bounty next to her. Hanna asked him to put in the Barbie *Nutcracker* video.

"Are you going to be okay?" he asked.

"Yes, Daddy," Hanna said without looking away from the television. When Ken left the living room a few minutes later, Hanna was watching the television, holding one of her new Barbie dolls.

Ken walked into his studio and turned on the lights. He wished he had natural light, but in late winter, that was scarce, so he made do. After moving the paintings around, he put the original portrait of Patrick on the easel and stared into the eyes as he tried to imagine what Patrick would have looked like when he was on stage. The image that had been so vibrant the day before had dulled somewhat, but he closed his eyes and concentrated, imagining Patrick on stage. When he hit play on the CD player without opening his eyes and heard Patrick's rich voice fill the room, the image in his mind began to sing. Then he opened his eyes, transferred that image to the canvas, and began to paint.

He worked for hours, only stopping from time to time to check on Hanna, make dinner, and to put Hanna to bed. As soon as she was asleep, he returned to the canvas, working late into the night without thinking of anything other than his work and Hanna. He was so engrossed in what he was doing he didn't realize he had an audience.

PATRICK stepped away from the window at the side of his house. For some reason, he'd only just discovered that if he looked out this particular window, he could see into Ken's studio. He'd been standing at the window for a while, watching as Ken worked. He couldn't see what he was painting and he wondered what had Ken so enthralled this late at night. Patrick had watched as Ken and Hanna hurried out of the house earlier. He'd gotten the box of dolls he'd found at small thrift stores around town and had been leaving the house to take them over when he'd seen Ken's ex-boyfriend pull up, so he'd waited until he left before setting the box down by their door. He'd waited for them to come home, and he'd heard Hanna's squeals of delight when she'd found the box. He had also heard her cough, and figured they must have been visiting the doctor. That had worried him, but Ken's relaxed stride had soothed his anxiety about Hanna. Over the past few months of watching Ken, he'd gotten pretty good at determining how he was feeling.

Like tonight—Patrick had watched Ken work in his studio, his body upright, arms flowing. Whatever Ken had been painting, he could see it was making him very happy. He'd thought about going outside to get a closer look, but he didn't want to stalk Ken. He liked him, and everything about his neighbor, and his daughter, fascinated him. There were times, like this evening, where the way he simply couldn't seem to move away from the window frightened him a little. He knew he was beginning to obsess over Ken, but the man was so nice, and he treated Patrick like a human being. Not many people had done that since the accident. Most people in town looked the other way when he came by. Patrick walked through his house, turning off the lights as he went, and then headed to his bedroom. He undressed and climbed into bed, but not without peering out his window so he could catch a glimpse of the light from Ken's window as it spilled over the snow in Ken's backyard.

Patrick closed his eyes, letting his imagination take over, and transported himself into Ken's studio. Ken continued working as Patrick approached him from behind. Ken didn't turn around and kept working until Patrick slipped his hands along Ken's side, tugging his shirt up. He felt Ken start for a fraction of a second and then begin to hum softly. In his mind he heard the tink of brushes being set aside, Ken's palette met the table in a clunk of wood on wood, and then Patrick tugged the paint-spattered shirt off, dropping it onto the drop cloths that covered the floor. Ken said nothing as Patrick stroked his smooth skin with a slowness that made Ken groan and Patrick's legs shake with anticipation. Ken shifted, leaning into him, and Patrick kissed along Ken's shoulder and up his neck. Patrick inhaled deeply, Ken's rich scent mixing with the paint in a way that went right to his head and his groin.

Patrick slid his hand down Ken's chest, wrapping his fingers around his cock as the Ken in his mind turned around, Patrick's hands sliding along his skin as he moved. Ken tugged off Patrick's shirt, then tilted his head slightly, their lips meeting in a kiss that didn't need the words Patrick couldn't utter. Patrick felt Ken's heart just as he knew Ken felt his. Being hugged close felt good and Patrick pressed his chest to Ken's. As they breathed, their skin rubbed ever so slightly, reminding them just how close they were to each other. In Patrick's mind, they slowly fell to the floor, the drop cloths becoming their bed. Clothes vanished with a thought, and then Ken's hands were everywhere, and Ken's lips were against his. The world shook as Patrick clamped his eyes closed. Then it was over, and Patrick floated for a few seconds before opening his eyes once again. Patrick opened the drawer in his nightstand and pulled out a towel that he used for cleanup before dropping it to the floor.

CHAPTER
Four

IT LOOKED like spring had finally arrived in northern Michigan. It was early May, and Patrick was working in the yard, clearing the last of winter's debris out of the bushes. He was careful not to disturb the sprouting bulbs as they reached for the spring sun. Patrick had seen Hanna and Ken a number of times over the past month, and they'd even asked him to dinner, which he really appreciated, even if Ken's cooking hadn't improved much. Patrick had taken some dinner over at least once a week, usually some of the "mac-cheese" that Hanna loved so much. He'd taken some over yesterday, but Hanna hadn't greeted him at the door the way she usually did. Instead, Ken had said she was sleeping, but he looked all worried, and Patrick wanted desperately to ask if she was all right. Instead, he'd stood there staring into Ken's eyes, hoping for some sort of answer, but all he'd gotten was more confused as anxious energy rolled off Ken.

So now he was outside working, watching Ken's house like a hawk for any sign of activity, but he saw nothing. Ken's car was parked out front, and he wanted to ask Ken about Hanna, he even had a note in his pocket all written, but he stayed away and kept working and watching.

"Patrick," a familiar voice called, and he looked up as Julianne strode toward him with a smile on her face. "I expected you to be in your shop," she teased, and Patrick gave her his best annoyed stare. "I know. On a day like this, you couldn't help being outside." Patrick leaned on his rake, and his eyes traveled to Ken's front door and then back to Julianne. She followed his gaze and then looked back at him. "So that's what you're doing out here." She glared at him, putting her hands on her hips. "Have you turned into a busybody?"

Patrick turned away, snorting slightly through his nose as he headed toward his front door. He knew she'd follow him, and sure enough, she did. Patrick found a pad and quickly scrawled his message. "*I'm worried about Hanna. When I took them over some dinner, Ken looked scared, and Hanna was asleep,*" he wrote, handing the paper to her before going to the front window, parting the curtains so he could peer out.

"You really are, aren't you?" Julianne asked as she placed her hand on his shoulder. "You really care for both of them."

Patrick nodded, wishing for the millionth time that he had his voice back even for a few minutes so he could tell her what he was feeling, but it took too long to write everything down, and he wasn't sure he could express what he wanted to anyway. Instead, he nodded as he let the curtain fall back into place. Patrick motioned her toward the kitchen, then followed her in and put on a pot of coffee before getting two mugs out of the cupboard. He also opened a tin of misshapen cookies that Hanna and Ken had brought by last week. He'd kept them wrapped tight, and while, like the others they brought over, they were a bit of a mess, they tasted good, and Patrick thought of Ken and Hanna whenever he ate one. He pushed the tin toward Julianne, who took one out and began to laugh. Patrick snatched the cookie out of her hand and put it back in the tin with a glare.

"She made those, didn't she?" Julianne asked as she tentatively reached for another cookie. "I'd like to meet them sometime." Patrick watched as Julianne took a bite of cookie and smiled. "So I have a question for you," she began as Patrick got the pot of coffee and filled both mugs. "You've been buying all kinds of things lately. Barbie dolls, tea sets, have they all been for her?" Patrick gave her his best "who else" look. "Have you told them yet?"

Patrick shook his head as he reached for the pad. "*I don't want them to know. I'm happy knowing I made Hanna smile,*" he wrote.

"You should really tell him," Julianne said as she sipped her coffee. "You really like and care for both of them. They deserve to know that."

Patrick shook his head violently and snatched back the pad. "*What if he...,*" Patrick began and then scratched it out. "*How could he...,*" he began again and then scratched it out one more time. "*He won't feel the same way,*" he finally scribbled and handed the pad to Julianne.

When she read the paper, Julianne's eyes went all gooey. Patrick had to stifle the urge to throw her out. "Sorry, but, Patrick, honey, what if he likes you too?" Julianne asked. "And don't roll your eyes at me again. It's becoming annoying." Julianne sipped from her mug with a small smile threatening to break out on her pink lips. "I know you've had it really hard since the accident, but there's no reason why Ken wouldn't like you." Julianne set down her mug, and Patrick stepped back from the counter. "Stop that," Julianne chastised. "I'm serious. You're an incredibly loving and caring man. Anyone you let get close to you can see that. But that's the problem—you won't let anyone close." Julianne glared at him. "Instead, you'd rather leave boxes of things on the front step for the daughter of the guy you like rather than just letting him know how you feel." Julianne picked up her mug again and grabbed another cookie. "Paddy, you know I love you, but you need to consider taking a chance. You can't keep yourself cooped up here all the time."

Patrick figured he could, and he scowled at her for using that ridiculous nickname. After snatching back the pad, he plopped it on the counter. "*I don't want to get hurt again,*" Patrick wrote and pushed the pad to Julianne before pulling it back again. "*You can understand that, can't you?*" he added.

"Of course I can," Julianne told him. "But if you don't take a chance, you'll never find out what could possibly happen. I know you've been in love, and I know you remember how wonderful it felt. You can feel that again if you allow yourself to."

Patrick heard what she was saying, but honestly, he didn't believe it. Ken was gorgeous, with his deep blue eyes and the face of the sexiest angel in heaven. He'd been spending much of the winter undressing Ken Brighton with his imagination, but the thought of approaching him, only to get his heart broken, was something he couldn't do.

"Think about it," Julianne said. She finished her coffee before walking toward the front door. "Stop by for dinner this weekend, okay?" Patrick nodded, and she hurried back, kissing him on the cheek before saying good-bye and leaving the house.

Patrick put the mugs in the sink and turned off the lights, then pulled on his gloves again before heading back outside. Patrick opened the door and stepped outside into the crisp spring air and heard Julianne's voice. Following the sound, he saw her standing beside Ken's car as he was almost literally throwing things in the trunk. "I'm Patrick's cousin, Julianne, and if there's anything we can do to help, don't hesitate to let us know." Patrick saw Julianne thrust a scrap of paper into Ken's hand.

"Thank you," Ken said with more than a hint of panic in his voice as he got in the car and closed the door. Patrick approached the car, standing next to Julianne as the engine started. Patrick looked in the back and saw Hanna in her seat, head slumped against the window. She looked like she might be asleep, but even through the glass, Patrick could see how frail and small she looked. Hanna was sick again, and Patrick gasped as the car pulled away from the curb, tires nearly screaming as it raced down the street.

Julianne turned to him and slapped him on the shoulder. "Why didn't you tell me that little girl was totally adorable?" She looked teary, and Patrick knew her huge heart was aching for Ken and Hanna, and she'd barely met them. Patrick shrugged and tried not to look like she'd just asked him the stupidest question on earth. "Sorry, but seeing her kicked in all the fears I've ever had about Todd."

Patrick nodded, turning his eyes to where Ken's car was turning onto the main road. He could kick himself for not going over and somehow finding out what was wrong. He'd known it and had done nothing.

"They're on their way to the hospital in Marquette. I heard him tell the little girl as he placed her in the car," Julianne said as she wiped her eyes. Patrick seemed rooted on the spot, worried about Hanna and aching at the glimpse of the panic he'd seen in Ken's eyes. Another slap brought him out of his thoughts, and he rubbed his shoulder. She might have been small, but Julianne packed a wallop.

"What," he mouthed, holding up his hands as he shrugged. He then stepped back to get out of the line of fire.

"Do you really like him?" Julianne asked, and Patrick thought for a second before nodding multiple times. "Then get your butt in the car and follow him. He's going to be alone at the hospital and worried sick. If you care, then you need to be there for him." She was practically yelling at him. "It's time to pull your head out of your butt and decide what you want." She poked him in the chest for emphasis. "You've wallowed in self-pity and isolation for two freakin' years." Julianne stomped toward her car. "I love ya, but you drive me crazy sometimes," Julianne said as she hurried back to give him a quick hug. Then she rushed away, and Patrick heard her sniff a few times as she got in the car.

Patrick watched her go, staring down the street, but not seeing anything at all. "Damn it," he swore before grabbing the rake from where he'd left it leaning against the house. He'd reached for it intending to go back to work, but instead he now carried it to the garage and put it away. Now that he'd decided, Patrick hurriedly turned out the lights and locked the house before rushing back to the garage and getting into his car. He was on the road toward Marquette within a matter of minutes.

He'd made the drive a million times, but never in ten minutes flat. Thankful he hadn't been pulled over, Patrick parked outside the hospital emergency room and hurried inside. "Can I help you?" the woman behind a glass window asked, and Patrick stopped cold. He began to motion for a pen and paper. "Are you having trouble breathing?" she asked, and Patrick took a deep breath to show her he wasn't. Reaching through the hole in the glass, he grabbed a pen and pad. "*I'm mute*," he wrote first. "*I'm looking for Ken Brighton and his daughter*." He handed the pad to her.

"You aren't here for yourself?" she asked, and Patrick shook his head. The woman looked relieved and began typing. "Please have a seat," she told him, and Patrick sat in the waiting area, glancing around him. A few minutes later, he was called, and he followed the woman through a set of doors that opened for him. They closed by themselves, and Patrick followed her down a hallway to a small room where Hanna lay in a bed. She looked so

81

tiny, with a mask over her nose and mouth, her eyes closed, her small body looking lost under all the covers.

Ken stood up, looking shocked, worried, and scared. "I thought she had the flu," Ken explained and began to cry. Patrick had no words of comfort. Those had been taken away, so he stepped closer and tugged Ken into a hug. He felt the other man stiffen at first, but then Ken's warm body melted to his and Patrick held him tighter. He wanted to say that everything would be okay, that the doctors would figure out what was happening and be able to help Hanna, but he couldn't. All Patrick could do was hold Ken as tightly as he could to let him know that he was there. Instead of using words, he had to use touch.

Patrick heard Hanna mumble, and he loosened his embrace, peering over Ken's shoulder. Hanna's eyes were open. Ken stepped away and turned to Hanna, sitting in the chair next to the bed and taking her tiny hand in his. "Patrick came to see how you are," Ken told her, and she nodded slightly before closing her eyes once again. "They don't know much right now," Ken told him quietly, anticipating his question. Ken stood up and motioned Patrick toward the chair. Patrick shook his head, but Ken motioned again. "She knows you're here."

Patrick reluctantly sat down and took Hanna's hand. She mumbled something softly under the mask, and Patrick felt her give his hand the slightest squeeze. Patrick lightly stroked the back of her hand with his thumb, looking at her, marveling at how quickly a six-year-old girl could steal his heart. He felt tears well in his eyes and he blinked them away until he looked at Ken and saw the same tears in his eyes. He was such a goner. Sitting in that chair with Hanna's hand in his, Patrick knew he'd given his heart to both of them. The walls he'd constructed to protect himself from the pain and barbs of the world cracked and threatened to crumble as he sat in the hospital chair.

"This must be Mr. Patrick," a woman said from the foot of Hanna's bed, and he looked up. "I'm Dr. Pierson. Hanna has told me a lot about you during her visits." The doctor began examining Hanna, removing the mask so she could look at her face and then placing it carefully over her mouth and nose once again. "We need to determine what's happening, so I've ordered some tests for tomorrow. We're going to move her into a room and make her as comfortable as we can."

"Thank you," Ken said softly. "I thought she had the flu," he added helplessly, and Patrick touched Ken lightly on the shoulder. He knew Ken was beating himself up over what had happened.

"I know you did, and a day or two wasn't going to make any difference. From what's on her chart, I would have suspected the same thing," the doctor said gently to Ken. "We'll find out what's happening, and we'll figure out a treatment plan if we need one. We're going to take a little blood now so we can get started, and then as soon as we get a room ready, we'll move her up there." The doctor prepared to leave, and Ken thanked her before walking around to the other side of the bed. Patrick began to stand up, but Ken motioned him back down as he took Hanna's other hand in his and stood on the far side of the bed, looking at his daughter. Ken's lips quivered, and his eyes filled with pain and fear. Patrick felt the same emotions welling inside him, but he couldn't begin to fathom what Ken was feeling.

Patrick knew how he'd felt when the doctors had told him he'd never talk or sing again. The next blow had come when he hadn't been able to prove them wrong. He'd thought his life was over, and more than once he'd simply wished he would die. Patrick had thought of ending it all, but in the end he'd withdrawn into himself and moved back home. If anything happened to Hanna, Patrick knew Ken would feel many of those same things, and his heart ached because he'd do anything to keep Ken from feeling so lost and alone.

They sat quietly for a long time, listening to Hanna breathe. Every now and then, Patrick gazed into her confused and terrified eyes. Patrick knew she'd been through this before, and he saw the fear in her eyes as she wondered if she was going to have to go through everything all over again. He had no practical idea of what Hanna had been through, but from the look in her eyes, as well as the helplessness in Ken's, Patrick knew it was some form of hell.

Dr. Pierson came back into the room. "We're going to move her to a room," Dr. Pierson said quietly from the foot of Hanna's bed, and Patrick stood up to give the people who'd followed her access to the bed. Ken stepped away as well, only letting go of Hanna's hand when they began to move her. The orderlies talked softly as they worked, and then they slowly rolled Hanna out of the little room and along the hallways. Ken walked behind her, and Patrick fell in next to him. Ken looked lost and scared. Without thinking, Patrick reached for Ken's hand and held it in his. The orderlies glanced at them, but Patrick met their gaze with a hard stare and they looked away and continued their work. When they reached the room, the orderlies set the bed in place and a nurse took over, making sure Hanna was settled.

"This is going to make her comfortable, but she'll sleep for hours," the nurse explained as she injected some medication into the IV line they'd put in earlier. Hanna's eyes drifted closed, and Ken held her hand once again.

"Ken," the doctor said as she walked into the room. She checked over everything before turning to him. "Hanna is going to sleep through the night. I want you to go home and get some rest. You know how the next few days are going to be, and you need to be strong for her. I know you want to stay, but there's nothing you can do except let her sleep. We'll call you if there's any change at all, I promise." She took Ken's hand in hers. "You need to rest."

"I need to be here with Hanna," Ken protested, and the doctor sighed, looking at Patrick for help, but all he could do was shrug. He wasn't in any position to convince Ken to do anything.

"Ken. Let this nice man take you home. Come back first thing in the morning, but you need to rest." This time there was an edge to her voice. "This can be a long process, you know that. Don't knock yourself out at the start of the race, because Hanna is going to need you for the long haul." Ken's expression softened, and he leaned over the bed, kissing Hanna on the forehead before stepping away from the bed. Patrick followed him, then turned back to wish Hanna a silent good-bye. Patrick followed a silent Ken through the hallways, Ken's body rigid with tension.

Night had fallen, and they stepped into the glow of large overhead lights as they emerged from the building and walked through the parking lot. Patrick led them to his car, and when Ken looked like he was going to continue, Patrick took his arm and guided Ken into his car. He wasn't going to let Ken drive home— he was too worried and distracted. To Patrick's surprise, Ken didn't put up a fight.

The drive home was made in complete silence, with only the sound of the road beneath the wheels. Ken stared blankly out the window the entire time, and Patrick drove, glancing over at him often. He knew that Ken was being torn apart with anxiety, and Patrick wanted to help but didn't know how. Finally, Patrick pulled up in front of Ken's house and the car drifted to a stop. Patrick got out and waited for Ken to do the same, watching from over the roof as Ken schlumped up the walk to his front door. Patrick closed the car door and turned toward his own house. He'd move his car later.

"Patrick," Ken said, and Patrick stopped walking. "I don't want to be alone." Patrick wasn't completely sure what Ken meant, but he walked back toward Ken's house and followed him inside.

The house seemed cold and quiet without Hanna to greet him with her squeals and hugs. Ken turned on a light and flopped down on the sofa with a soft sigh before leaning forward so he could bury his face in his hands. Patrick sat down next to him, the words to say that it would be okay forming on his lips, but all that came out was a series of soft grunts that sounded like nothing. He could make some sounds, but not enough to make himself understood. So he gave up, pulling Ken to him and saying what he needed to with his body and hands.

"Is that your way of reassuring me?" Ken asked, and Patrick nodded, hugging him a little tighter. "I shouldn't have waited. I know what the doctor said, but I still should have taken her in right away."

Patrick smoothed his hand over Ken's hair, unable to reassure him any other way. There were times when he felt inadequate, but this wasn't one of them. Anyone could say the words to try to comfort, but holding Ken in his arms, even if only to comfort him, felt wonderful, and he'd sit like this all night if Ken would let him. "Are you hungry?" Ken asked, and Patrick thought for a few minutes, trying to remember the last time he'd eaten. It had definitely been hours, so he let his arms slip away and stood up, then walked toward the kitchen to see what Ken had in the house.

He opened the refrigerator and then began looking in the cupboards. Patrick expected Ken to follow him, but he heard no footsteps. Figuring Ken needed to be alone for a while, Patrick found some bread and various lunch meats in one of the refrigerator drawers. He was also able to find a few other items, and began making sandwiches. Then he found the plates and glasses. After pouring some milk, Patrick carried a plate and glass into the living room and set it on the coffee table in front of Ken. After returning to the kitchen to get his own plate, Patrick joined Ken, sitting next to him and giving him a small nudge with his elbow to try to get him to eat.

Eventually Ken picked up the sandwich and took a bite before setting it down again. "When I first got Hanna a few years ago, I never imagined how a tiny life could mean so much to me." Ken sat back, and Patrick ate as he watched Ken stare at the walls. "She was a little slip of a thing, but she had so much energy. I knew as soon as I met her that she was meant for me to love."

Patrick wanted to ask all kinds of questions, but he lacked the ability, and he didn't want to interrupt Ken by writing things down, so he simply listened.

"Would you like to see a picture?" Ken stood up without waiting for an answer. Patrick took another bite of his sandwich as Ken pulled open a cabinet drawer and pulled out a photo album. When Ken returned to the couch, he opened it and showed Patrick the first pages. "She wasn't quite three when I first got her. I had to foster her at first, but then a year later I adopted her." Ken smiled, his fingers brushing over the photographs of the little girl in her pink shirt smiling for the camera. She was adorable, with big eyes and wild hair. "I met Mark a little while later, and we were going to raise her together, but you know how that turned out."

Patrick nodded. He wished he could say that Ken was better off without his self-centered boyfriend. Instead, he rolled his eyes to no one and took another bite of sandwich. Ken turned the page on the photo album, and Patrick picked up Ken's plate, handing it to him insistently.

"You'd think you were my mother," Ken teased before taking a small bite and then setting the plate back on the table. "Happy?" Patrick shook his head, and Ken huffed but began to eat while Patrick looked at the pictures of Hanna. There was one of her holding a fishing pole with a tiny fish on the end of the line. Patrick saw the delighted look on her face and he could almost hear her squeal of delight as she'd reeled the fish out of the water. There were also pictures of her riding a pony and on a carousel. Patrick turned the page and saw that Hanna had gotten a little older, with pictures of her swimming in what looked like a pool. There were also pictures of her on Christmas morning opening presents and holding them up so Ken could see them.

Patrick turned the page again, and there were pictures of her outside playing. Then the pictures shifted, some of them showing her in hospital beds with a hat on her head. Patrick needed no explanation as to when they were taken. Ken carefully closed the album and set it aside. "Someday I know I'll be able to look at those, but I can't right now." Patrick nodded again and finished off his sandwich before prodding Ken one more time to eat. "Will you stay with me?" Ken asked, and Patrick widened his eyes in surprise. He wasn't sure that was a good idea, but he nodded anyway. Ken finally finished his sandwich, and Patrick took the plates and glasses to the kitchen, setting them in the sink before cleaning everything else up. When he returned to Ken's living room, he saw him still sitting on the sofa. It looked as though he hadn't moved the entire time Patrick had been gone.

Patrick knew he needed to get Ken to bed and to sleep. If Ken stayed up worrying, he wouldn't be any help to Hanna or anyone else. Without knowing what else to do, Patrick extended his hand, and when Ken accepted it, Patrick led him upstairs.

Patrick knew he probably should not be doing this. He'd watched and dreamed of being with Ken, but this was not how he'd ever imagined it. In his imagination, he'd always pictured them happy. The first time he was with Ken like this was supposed to be magical. He reminded himself that nothing intimate was going to happen—it couldn't. This was about as unsexy a situation as he could think of. Hanna was in the hospital, and Ken was almost totally distraught.

When Patrick reached the top of the stairs, he looked through each open door until he found Ken's room and then led him inside. The unmade bed and clothes lying on the floor spoke of the distraction and rushed nature of Ken's recent life. Patrick kept himself busy picking up the clothes and dropping them into a basket in the corner while Ken undressed and climbed into bed. Patrick saw Ken's eyes close, and he turned out the light. Figuring he would sleep on the sofa downstairs, Patrick turned to leave, but Ken touched his arm. "Don't go," he whispered, and Patrick took a deep breath, holding it for a few seconds before releasing it and walking around to the other side of the bed.

Patrick toed off his shoes and stripped to his underwear in the dark room. Then he lifted the covers, climbed between the cool sheets, and settled on the mattress. He stared up at the ceiling, a little afraid to move. Ken's breathing was nearly deafening in the otherwise silent room, and Ken's heat traveled along the bedding to warm Patrick. Turning to look at his bedmate, Patrick got a whiff of his deep, rich scent, and he had to stifle the groan that threatened. There was no doubt about it: Patrick was in hell, especially when his body reacted to Ken's proximity with gusto. He began thinking unsexy thoughts and reminded himself that the only reason he was here was because Hanna was in the hospital and Ken was worried out of his mind. That chilled things quickly, but they only heated up when Ken shifted on the bed next to him. In the darkness, an arm settled over his chest, and then Ken was pressing close to his side.

"Just hold me, Patrick," Ken whispered. Patrick rolled onto his side, and Ken settled right against him, their bodies fitting like two perfect pieces of a jigsaw puzzle. "It's been a while and…."

"I know," Patrick mouthed silently, not caring if he could say the words out loud or not. Wrapping Ken in his arms, Patrick hugged him tightly. If he only got this one chance to hold Ken in his arms, he'd take it and remember it for the rest of his life. Patrick had no illusions that this was more than just Ken needing comfort after a traumatic day, and when they got up in the morning, everything would change in the light of day.

"You're a good friend," Ken murmured, and Patrick held his breath at the unexpected pain those simple words caused. He didn't want to be Ken's friend. He wanted so very much more, but he couldn't tell him that, not now and not in the dark, so Patrick had to be content with holding Ken as he felt and heard him drift off to sleep. Patrick spent quite a long time listening to Ken breathe as he lay wide awake long after Ken rolled over and Ken's warm back pressed to his chest. Eventually Patrick's eyes drifted closed and he fell asleep, but not for very long.

When Patrick woke in the middle of the night, the clock on Ken's side of the bed read 4:32, and he was alone in the bed. Wondering where Ken was, Patrick got up and slipped into his pants before wandering through the house. He saw light glowing from downstairs and followed it to the back of the house into what had to be Ken's studio. Patrick found Ken standing in front of an easel in his underwear working diligently on a canvas. He could see Ken shivering as he continued to work feverishly, as though the world didn't exist.

Patrick moved around behind him to where he could see what Ken was painting. Hanna stared out from the canvas, her eyes twinkling, the puffy pink hat that Patrick had given her on her head. Her arm was near the edge of the canvas, a snowball in her mittened hand, ready to be thrown. Patrick smiled, because even though the objective of the snowball wasn't in the painting, Patrick knew it was most likely him or Ken. Patrick began to shiver, and he lightly touched Ken's bare shoulder. His skin was cold, and Patrick wondered how long Ken had been down here working like this.

"I remembered our snowball fight a few months ago, and I needed to get Hanna's expression captured before I forgot it," Ken said as he continued applying paint to Hanna's rosy cheeks.

"I get images, but sometimes they don't last long," Ken said as he dabbed his brush in more paint. "I dreamed about this day, and I couldn't let it go," Ken said as he continued working. Patrick figured he could leave and Ken would hardly know he'd left. Moving away, Patrick turned to leave the studio. The soft sounds of Ken's work ceased, and Patrick looked over his shoulder. Ken stood poised with his brush near the canvas, not moving, staring back at him. He didn't move for a while, and then slowly he lowered his brush, setting it on the paint-spattered table behind him. The palette followed, and Ken still stared as though he were trying to impress something onto his brain.

Patrick began feeling a little uncomfortable under the scrutiny. Ken's gaze was so intense, Patrick had to look away. Taking a quick glance around the studio, he saw canvases leaning against walls. In some places, multiple canvases leaned one on top of each other. Some had been painted, but the ones he could see were blank. Patrick walked back to where Ken continued staring. He touched Ken's arm and then took his hand, lightly guiding him out of the room. Ken pulled away and hurriedly rushed around, putting lids on paint and dropping brushes into cups. Patrick was shivering again by the time he'd had enough and took Ken by the hand again, leading him out of the studio and up the stairs. Ken flipped the lights off, and they made much of the trip in near darkness.

In Ken's bedroom, Patrick got Ken under the covers before climbing in bed himself. Ken curled right next to him, his skin cold and his feet—God, Patrick shivered when Ken's feet found his. Patrick pulled Ken tighter, letting their heat mingle as he slowly warmed them both. "Thanks for taking care of me," Ken mumbled, and Patrick figured he was already half asleep. Patrick closed his eyes as well and soon drifted off with Ken's now warm back pressed to his chest. Patrick had few illusions that this would last in the morning.

THE next time Patrick woke, it was to Ken stirring in bed. He opened his eyes, peered over at the clock, and realized that only a few hours had passed. "Would you take me back to the hospital?" Ken asked, and Patrick got out of bed, knowing that what he'd feared last night had come to pass. Patrick dressed as he looked around for a way to communicate. He found a piece of paper on the nightstand, and Ken handed him a pencil.

"I'm going home to change clothes. I'll meet you at my car in ten minutes," Patrick wrote before handing Ken the paper and then hurrying out of the room and down the stairs. He found his coat in the living room, shrugged it on, and then hurried outside and down the street. Inside his house, Patrick hurried to his room and tugged off his clothes, grabbing the closest things at hand. In his bathroom, he shaved in a hurry and cleaned up as best he could before pulling on his clothes, stepping into a pair of shoes, and then grabbing his coat as he hurried back out the door.

Ken stood by his car, waiting for him. Patrick unlocked the doors, and they got inside. He started the engine and took off toward the highway, fastening his seat belt before he reached the stop sign at the end of the street.

"Thank you for last night," Ken said when they reached the highway, and Patrick glanced over at him briefly. "I really appreciated you being there." Ken shifted in his seat. "Without you I wouldn't have slept at all, I know that. You were a good friend."

There it was again—he was a friend. Patrick needed to get that through his head and stop all his wishing and dreaming. Ken wasn't going to see him as anything more than that, no matter how much he might wish for it. Patrick continued driving, trying not to let what he was feeling show on his face. Instead, he concentrated on how good and right it had felt to hold Ken in his arms. He'd told himself last night that he might only get the one chance to do that, and it looked like he was probably right.

Patrick pushed all those thoughts aside as he continued driving. There were more important people to worry about, like Hanna. His hurt feelings didn't really matter in the long run, anyway.

By the time they arrived at the hospital, Patrick had his feelings under control. He strode behind Ken as they negotiated the hospital corridors toward Hanna's room. As they approached her door, the nurse was just leaving. "How is she?"

"Basically the same, but her fever is down a bit," the nurse answered. "She's still asleep, but hopefully she'll wake up soon."

Ken nodded and went inside while Patrick stood outside, giving him a few minutes alone with his daughter. When he entered, Hanna appeared to be awake, her eyes fluttering. Ken held Hanna's hand, and Patrick slowly moved into the room, locking his gaze on hers. At least they'd removed the oxygen mask and just had the tube running to Hanna's nose so Patrick could see her slight smile. Then she rolled her head to look at her dad.

"Am I gonna be bald again?" Hanna asked.

Ken shrugged slightly. "I don't know what kind of treatment will be needed. But if you are, we'll get as many pretty hats as we can find."

The nurse they'd seen earlier came in to take some more blood. Hanna didn't flinch when she stuck in the needle. "You're such a good little girl," the nurse said to Hanna, smiling as she finished up what she needed to do. "The doctor will be in soon, and I'll get these down to the lab." The nurse left after stroking Hanna's cheek lightly. "Rest if you can, sweetheart," she added before leaving the room.

Ken sighed, and Patrick looked around before pulling a chair up to the bed. He wondered if he was interfering and should go home, but Hanna reached for him, taking his hand in hers. "It's okay, Mr. Patrick, I'm a big girl."

"I know you are. But even big girls shouldn't have to be in the hospital," Ken said, and Patrick nodded. *No girls should have to be in the hospital, big or not,* he wanted to tell her, but he just held her hand instead. Sometimes being mute really sucked. And this was definitely one of those times. All he could do was hold Hanna's hand and smile when she looked at him. But from the way she held onto him in return, maybe that was enough. They sat quietly while Hanna dozed.

The doctor stepped into the room, motioning for Ken to follow her. Ken stood up, and Patrick watched him, silently asking if Ken wanted him to stay here or go with him. "Please keep her company," Ken told him, and Patrick nodded and settled back in the chair. Hanna opened her eyes when Ken had left, looking for him for a second before settling her gaze on Patrick. He rubbed her hand lightly to soothe her and watched the door for Ken's return.

Hanna had drifted back to sleep by the time Ken stepped back into the room, looking a bit shell-shocked. Patrick gently settled Hanna's hand on the blanket, her eyes remaining closed, and he got up, following Ken back out into the hall. "The doctor said the cancer has returned. They're going to try a different treatment, but they have to get her stronger before they can start it." Ken swallowed hard, and Patrick had a million questions, but he had to wait for Ken to continue. Patrick's hands clenched into fists as frustration welled inside him at his enforced silence. "She's going to be here for a while… and there's no guarantee."

Patrick nodded before hurrying to the nurse's station and motioning for a pad and paper. A confused nurse looked at him like he was crazy.

"He isn't able to speak, and he's asking for a pen and paper," Ken explained from behind him with a glare at the nurse, who instantly looked contrite as she rummaged around on the desk before handing him a note pad and pen.

"*What about a bone marrow transplant?*" Patrick scrawled.

"She isn't a candidate," Ken answered. "The doctor gave a reason, but it was difficult to understand. She's hopeful that this treatment will work, but it's going to be harder on her than the last one." Ken bit his lip as he looked back at Hanna's room. He looked about ready to break down, and Patrick tugged him into his arms, holding Ken tight. It was the only comfort he could offer. "I don't know what I'll do if I lose her," Ken whispered into Patrick's ear, and Patrick could hear the tears threatening in Ken's voice. Patrick felt his own tears start to fill his eyes, but he had to push them back. Ken tightened his grip for a few seconds before stepping back, wiping his eyes as he took a deep breath. "Thank you for everything."

Patrick nodded, and Ken turned and walked back into Hanna's room. Patrick followed. Hanna was awake, and Patrick took her hand, stroking her skin lightly before leaning over the bed to kiss her on the forehead. Then he walked around the bed to where Ken sat, touching his hand lightly to say good-bye before picking up his coat and walking to the door.

"Bye, Mr. Patrick," Hanna said softly, and he lifted his hand. "Will you come back soon?" Her voice sounded so rough and weak that Patrick felt the tears threaten to well again. Nodding, he waved slightly before leaving the room and walking down the hallway. Patrick followed the signs to the lobby and then left the hospital, heading toward his car.

THE drive back toward Pleasanton gave Patrick a chance to think, and as he approached town, he drove to Julianne's instead of going home. He hoped like hell she wasn't at work, and breathed a sigh of relief when he pulled up in front of her house. The front door opened as he was coming up the walk, and Patrick's cousin, Todd, rushed down the walk, his little legs flying. Patrick hurried to meet him and scooped the little scamp into his arms. "Unca Patwick," he said, giggling, as Patrick was hugged to within an inch of his life. He carried Todd up the walk and into the house, closing the door behind them. Julianne met them in the hallway looking all stern.

"You'll catch cold if you run outside without a coat," she scolded Todd, who looked contrite for a few seconds before hugging Patrick once again. "Would you like something to eat?" Julianne asked as Patrick carried Todd down the hallway. Todd squirmed to get down, and as soon as Patrick set him on his feet, he raced into the kitchen, then returned with one of his trucks that he had to show his uncle.

"Mommy got dis for me," he pronounced proudly before running the car on the floor, making vroom-vroom and brake-screech sounds. Patrick settled on the floor as well, sailing cars across the floor with him. Julianne worked at the counter, preparing lunch.

"Toddy, you need to wash up," Julianne said, and Todd rushed out of the room toward the bathroom. Patrick followed him and helped Todd wash and dry his hands. Then he did the same before leaving the bathroom. Todd was already in his seat, legs swinging back and forth as he waited for Julianne to bring him his lunch. She fixed him a plate and set it down along with a sippy cup. Patrick took the chair next to Todd's, and Julianne brought two plates to the table, then sat down on the opposite side of her son. "What brings you by?" Julianne asked. "As if I didn't know." She pushed a pad and pen over to Patrick.

"*Hanna went into the hospital yesterday,*" Patrick wrote. "*The cancer has come back and she is going to need more treatment.*" He passed Julianne the pad.

"Any news on her prognosis?" Julianne asked, and Patrick shrugged, shaking his head. He took a bite of chicken salad and helped Todd with his chicken nuggets, giving him a stern look when he began playing with his food. Julianne could scold him, but all it took was a look from Patrick and he instantly behaved. "Something else happened, didn't it?" Julianne pressed, and Patrick nodded.

"*I brought Ken home from the hospital and he didn't want to be alone, so I stayed with him last night,*" Patrick wrote, and then he stopped for a second before deciding to tell her what he could. "*He said I was a great friend.*" He underlined "friend" and then pushed it toward Julianne with a small huff.

"You stayed with him?" Julianne asked once she'd read the note. "In the same bed?" she stage-whispered, and Patrick nodded before taking back the pad.

"*I just held and comforted him,*" he wrote. "*Nothing more,*" he wrote defensively, if that was possible. "*His daughter is in the hospital. It wouldn't have been right, even though I wanted to.*" Patrick passed the pad back to her. She read it and nodded.

"Is it the friend part that's bothering you?" she asked, and Patrick nodded vehemently. "Please," she said. "He's probably all messed up and in a really weird place. I bet he has no idea what he's feeling right now. You weren't expecting a sudden declaration of love, were you?" she added, and Patrick shook his head. "Then don't worry about it. You were a good friend and you care. He'll come to see that if you let him."

Patrick nodded slowly before returning to his lunch. They sat quietly, both of them eating and keeping an eye on Todd. Once they were done, Patrick helped her clear the dishes and then spent much of the afternoon playing with his cousin and wondering about Hanna and Ken.

CHAPTER
Five

SPRING was definitely in full swing and summer just around the corner as Ken brought Hanna home for the first time in weeks. She'd had a number of treatments, but there wasn't much more they could do until Hanna got stronger again, so he'd asked if he could bring her home. After pulling up in front of the house, Ken stopped the car and helped Hanna out. She stepped slowly up the walk, looking at everything around her. The trees had leafed out, and there were flowers blooming everywhere. Ken knew she wanted to look, and he closed his car door before taking her hand and leading Hanna through the yard. He hadn't had time to tend to anything in the yard and yet every bed was neat and weed-free. Ken had noticed it before, and he strongly suspected that Patrick had been taking care of things for him, but he'd never seen him in the yard, and the one time he'd asked him, Patrick had simply shrugged.

"Can I pick some flowers?" Hanna asked, and Ken smiled and nodded, letting her do whatever she wanted. Regardless of what the doctors said, Ken felt his hope fading a little more each day. After each treatment, Hanna seemed to be getting weaker, and the recovery time longer and longer. So if she wanted to pick spring flowers, she could pick anything she wanted. Ken found himself thinking that this could be the last spring his precious daughter saw, and if it was, he intended to make it the best one possible for her. Thoughts like that had come to him a lot lately.

Ken sat on the garden bench near the house and watched as Hanna slowly moved through the yard, wearing her favorite pink hat. It didn't matter to her if it was for winter or spring, and if she wanted to wear it, Ken wasn't going to say no. "Patrick," Hanna called, and she stopped working and carried her fistful of flowers over to where he stood on the sidewalk. He lifted her into his arms and held her like she was a precious object. Patrick walked with her to where Ken waited for them. Patrick had visited both of them many times in the hospital, and Hanna had always looked forward to each and every time he stuck his head in her room. So had Ken, for that matter.

"Thank you for taking care of the yard," Ken said. This time he wasn't asking, and Patrick colored slightly, but at least he didn't deny it.

"Will you stay for lunch?" Hanna asked, and Patrick nodded before pointing to his house. Ken watched as he pantomimed with Hanna, and then she squealed and hugged Patrick tight. "You made mac-cheese for me?" Hanna asked, and Patrick nodded before setting Hanna on her feet and then hurrying through the yard and down the sidewalk.

"Let's go inside. Patrick will join us in a few minutes," Ken explained, taking Hanna's hand.

Ken led her inside and helped Hanna get a vase for her flowers. He filled it with water and was placing the flowers in the middle of the table when he heard Hanna open the front door. Moments later, Hanna came into the kitchen with Patrick right behind her, carrying a steaming casserole dish. He'd obviously just taken it out of the oven. Ken placed a cloth on the table, and Patrick set down the hot dish. Then Ken got plates, cups, and utensils while Hanna got settled in her place. He and Patrick joined her at the table, with Ken putting a small amount of the perfectly gooey macaroni dish on Hanna's plate.

She blew on her plate, waiting impatiently for her mac-cheese to cool before taking a tentative bite. Hanna hadn't eaten a great deal in quite a while. The treatments tended to take away her appetite. Ken hated having to nearly beg Hanna to eat, but whenever Patrick came to the hospital, he'd always brought a treat for Hanna that she ate readily, usually something sweet. The doctor would have been angry if she had known, but Ken had simply been grateful that Hanna was eating anything. After a while, Patrick had taken to bringing him treats as well. Ken took a bite of the macaroni, the rich cheese sliding down his throat.

"This is wonderful. Thank you." When Ken had texted Patrick that he and Hanna were coming home, he hadn't intended for him to provide lunch, but he should have known he would anyway. Ken watched as Hanna ate slowly but steadily before shifting his gaze to Patrick. He didn't know exactly when it had happened, but over the last six weeks or so, his fascination with Patrick had begun to turn into something else.

"Good," Hanna said as she reached for her glass of milk, smiling at Patrick before continuing to eat.

"You've been a godsend this entire time, and I don't know how to thank you," Ken told Patrick, and he saw the silent man blush, nod quickly, and then look away. There were times when Patrick was so expressive, and times, like right now, that Ken wished he could easily ask what Patrick was thinking. He seemed so closed and cut off sometimes. Ken figured that was probably normal for a person who had lost his ability to speak, having lost the method used most to communicate. Ken knew he needed to explain what he was feeling to Patrick. He deserved to know, and there had been times over the past weeks that he'd seen glimpses of what he thought might be reciprocal feelings from Patrick.

While they'd been fleeting, he'd seen them more than once, especially when Patrick thought Ken wasn't looking.

Hanna finished her helping, and Ken gave her a little more, which she ate as well, to Ken's delighted surprise. "Can I go play?" she asked, sliding out of her seat and onto the floor.

"As long as you're quiet," Ken answered. "You remember what the doctor said."

"Daddy…," Hanna whined slightly before walking out of the kitchen. Ken heard her go upstairs and then come back down again. Turning around, he caught a glimpse of her carrying her art set toward the living room.

Ken smiled and returned his attention to Patrick. For a second, he caught a glimpse of Patrick's intense gaze, with a touch of fire in his eyes that made Ken shiver with excitement. The look didn't last long, because Patrick looked down at his plate almost immediately. "Patrick, I think there's something we need to talk about," Ken began, and then the doorbell rang. Ken groaned and stood up as he heard the front door open.

"Uncle Mark," Hanna said, and Ken walked into the hall, where Mark was releasing Hanna from a hug.

"This is a surprise," Ken said as he got a hug of his own. "I wasn't expecting you."

"You said when you called that Hanna was coming home today, so I had to stop by and see how my best girl was doing," Mark answered cheerfully, with a huge smile and a warm look in his eyes.

"We're just having some lunch. You're welcome to join us," Ken offered as Hanna closed the door. He led Mark into the kitchen and saw Patrick at the sink. "This is our neighbor, Patrick," Ken said.

"I remember," Mark said as Patrick held out his hand. "I'm Mark."

Patrick shook the offered hand before turning to Ken for a few seconds. All Ken saw was confusion and even a touch of hurt in Patrick's eyes. Then he held up his hand as he headed out of the room. Ken heard Hanna saying good-bye, and a few seconds later, the front door opened and closed. Ken groaned on the inside because he had really wanted to talk to Patrick. He had so many things he needed to say to him, but it was going to take time. He'd finally begun to come to terms with how he felt about Patrick, that his feelings were more than just friendship, and he wanted to be able to tell him and to confirm if those glimpses he kept getting were real or imagined. Covering his disappointment, Ken sighed softly. "Are you hungry?"

Mark shook his head and moved closer. "Not for food," he whispered with raised eyebrows.

"Mark, it's been months," Ken stammered, stepping back slightly. They'd had lunch a few times, and he'd been up to visit Hanna in the hospital, but up till now, Mark hadn't given him any indication that he'd wanted to get back together. "What's going on?" Ken asked in a whisper.

"I was a fool, Ken. I shouldn't have walked away. I was selfish and self-centered, and I realize now that I walked out on the best thing to ever happen to me at the time when you needed me most. I was so stupid not to have stood by you and realized that you loved me too. I thought that with the way you lavished your attention on Hanna that you didn't have time for me or want me anymore. I know I was wrong, and I know I hurt you. Can you find it in your heart to forgive me?" Mark asked quietly, and Ken felt his heart leap slightly.

"I missed you too," Ken confessed as his head spun. He had never anticipated that Mark would want back into his life after all these months. "But you hurt me badly, and I can't just switch my heart on and off." Truth be told, Ken had moved on, and he wasn't sure he ever wanted to go back to where he'd been.

"I don't want an answer from you today." Mark stepped closer once again, this time leaning close and then placing a light kiss on Ken's lips. "I really did miss you, and I'm truly sorry for being such a total ass." Mark backed away, and Ken licked his lips slightly.

"Why now, Mark?" Ken asked as his head swam just a little bit. Mark had always been able to easily touch his heart, and now was no exception. Ken had really thought that he was over Mark. When they'd first met for lunch, Ken had expected some sort of hurt to surface, but it hadn't. He'd been contented and pleased to spend some time with Mark, but he hadn't felt any heartache or even hurt. What he couldn't figure out was why Mark's light kiss left a tingling on his lips and a zing sliding up his spine. He didn't get it, and he needed some time to think.

"I never forgot about either Hanna or you. It took me a while to realize that when I'd left, I was leaving my family behind." Mark's voice caught slightly in his throat.

"But you've had months…," Ken began. He and Hanna were moving on, and this seemed to throw all that he thought he felt into disarray.

"I know," Mark agreed. "I was a total fool, okay, and I love you. It took me longer than it should have to realize how much I love both you and Hanna. You're both my family and my life." Mark took Ken's hands in his, squeezing them lightly as he rubbed Ken's skin with his thumbs. "Don't let my stupidity ruin a chance at happiness for all of us." Mark looked so plaintive and earnestly hurt that Ken couldn't tell him what he wanted to say. The words got caught in his throat, and he found himself nodding.

"You have to give me some time," Ken told him.

"That's all I could ever ask," Mark said. After releasing Ken's hands, Mark moved toward the kitchen door, then hurried back. Mark cupped Ken's cheeks in his hands and kissed him hard, full on the mouth, with enough energy to nearly fry Ken's brain. Then he stepped back, both of them breathing deeply, and without another word, he left the room. "I'll call you real soon," Mark said with a happy grin as he stuck his head in the doorway. Before Ken could react, Mark was gone, and he heard him saying good-bye to Hanna. Following the sound of their voices, Ken saw Mark hug Hanna tightly before kissing her on the cheek. Then he waved to both of them and left the house seeming to float on air.

Ken cleaned up the kitchen, placing the remaining food in the refrigerator and the dishes in the dishwasher. He was so confused. Mark would be the easy decision—he was known, and it would be easy to integrate him back into their lives and into Ken's heart. But he wasn't sure he wanted to. Mark never looked at him the way Patrick did when he thought Ken wasn't looking. Ken knew Mark cared for him; there was little doubt in Ken's mind that Mark was sincere. What Ken kept wondering was what he really wanted, and when he asked himself, all he got was that he didn't know. "Can we go outside, Daddy?" Hanna asked as he was finishing up.

"Would you like to go for a walk?" he asked, and Hanna nodded. "Then go get your jacket, and we'll spend some time in the fresh air." Hanna hurried away, and Ken got his jacket. After putting it on, he made sure Hanna was properly dressed. It might be spring, but she needed to remain warm. Once he was satisfied, Ken took Hanna's hand and they left the house.

Hand in hand, they walked slowly through the neighborhood as people enjoyed the lovely spring weather. "How are you doing?" Mrs. Krantz at the end of the block asked as she approached, taking off her gardening gloves.

"I'm fine," Hanna answered with a slight gleam in her eye that Ken hadn't seen in a while. "I still have to wear hats, though."

Mrs. Krantz leaned close to Hanna. "It's very pretty. Where did you get it?"

"It was a gift," Hanna explained with a smile, "but I don't know who gave it to me."

"Well, it's very pretty," Mrs. Krantz said as she straightened up, and Hanna thanked her as they continued on their way. Nearly everyone they encountered asked Hanna how she was doing. The people Ken didn't know, which seemed to be a lot of them, introduced themselves before talking to Hanna. They all seemed to ask the same questions. Some brought out cookies for her. A few gave her some flowers from their yard, which Hanna held onto as they continued their walk.

As they approached Patrick's house, Ken expected to see him out in his yard, but the house looked closed up tight and no one was around. "Can I go knock?" Hanna asked, and Ken guided her up the walk, lifting Hanna so she could ring the bell. No one came to the door, though. Hanna knocked, but the door remained closed, with only the sound of the breeze in their ears. They left Patrick's small front porch and headed down the walk. Hanna kept turning around to see if Patrick had come to the door, but they walked the rest of the way home without seeing their neighbor. "Is he mad at me?" Hanna asked as they approached their front door, once again looking for Patrick.

"No, honey. He probably had things to do," Ken explained even as the hurt expression on Patrick's face as he left flashed into Ken's mind. There was something bothering Patrick, Ken could sense it, but he couldn't ask Patrick what was bothering him right now, and Hanna needed to lie down for a while. After opening the front door, Ken lifted Hanna into his arms, and she curled against him, still holding her flowers. Ken closed the door and then took Hanna up to her room, setting her flowers on the dresser before getting her ready for a nap. By the time Ken got her jacket and shoes off and her blanket covering her, Hanna was asleep. Ken watched her for a few minutes before picking up the flowers and heading downstairs.

After placing the flowers in the vase with the ones Hanna had picked earlier, Ken wandered through to his studio. He hadn't painted in weeks, but the turmoil in his mind drove him to seek out paint and canvas. The portrait of Hanna had been finished, and he was close to finishing the one of Patrick singing and the full-length study that he'd started weeks earlier. Ken wasn't sure what he wanted to do and lifted a blank canvas into his easel. He thought of doing a portrait of Mark, and wondered why in all the time they'd been together, he'd never painted one. Closing his eyes, he brought up an image and solidified it in his mind before opening his eyes and getting to work.

IT WASN'T working. Hours later, Hanna was still asleep and the painting he'd been working on looked like a bunch of blotches. He couldn't find a direction, and the image in his head kept shifting. Stepping back, he looked at what he'd done, and his eyes widened. He'd been painting a portrait of Mark, but what he'd done so far looked more like Patrick. He lifted the canvas off his easel, leaned it against the wall, and then set the singing Patrick on the easel. As soon as he did, everything came into focus. Ken fumbled with his CD player and found one of Patrick's recordings.

As soon as the music began, Ken saw the image he needed in his mind's eye. Patrick stood on stage wearing the clothes he wore to work in the yard. One song ended, and as another began, the image in his mind began to sing, and Ken got to work.

His hands flew as though they had a mind of their own. He now knew exactly what he wanted to achieve and he was determined to finish. The last details of the painting that had been so hard for him earlier went in with an ease that was almost too good to be true. By the time the CD stopped playing, Ken had set the now finished painting aside to dry.

"Daddy," he heard from the other room.

"I'm in here," he told Hanna, and she wandered into the studio, rubbing her eyes. "Did you have a good nap, sweetheart?" Ken lifted her into his arms, and Hanna rested her head against his shoulder. Ken carefully closed his paints and put his brushes in thinner to clean a little later. He left the studio and carried Hanna through the house. They ended up in the living room, and he sat in one of the large chairs with Hanna on his lap, curled into his arms, as he turned on the television, and they watched cartoons together for the rest of the afternoon.

"What do you want for dinner?" Ken asked as the room began to dim. They had moved to the sofa, but every time he'd gotten up to leave, she'd moved closer. Ken wasn't going to begrudge her any attention he could lavish on her, so he stayed and watched cartoons that threatened to turn his mind to mush.

"Mac-cheese with Patrick," Hanna answered, and Ken sighed. "He makes the best mac-cheese."

"I know, honey, and we can check to see if he's home, but he may be gone." Ken still had things he wanted to talk over with him. Hanna got up and hunted up her jacket, then stood by the door waiting for Ken. Deciding it wasn't worth the fight, he got his own jacket and held Hanna's hand as they walked to Patrick's. The house was dark, and there didn't appear to be anyone home. Hanna insisted on ringing the bell and swore she could hear someone inside, but there were no lights and no one answered. "Let's go home and I'll heat up some dinner for you," Ken said, taking her hand and leading Hanna home. "We'll probably see him tomorrow." They stepped down the walk. Ken turned back when they reached the sidewalk, and he thought he might have seen the curtains on one of the front windows move, but he wasn't sure, and he certainly didn't say anything to Hanna. He hoped Patrick wasn't avoiding them for some reason and passed the movement off as nothing.

When they got home, Ken made Hanna some dinner and ate a little himself before putting her to bed. Ken read her a story, and once Hanna was asleep, Ken returned to his studio and got back to work. He'd already given up on the portrait of Mark and begun work on the large, full-sized painting of Patrick. He took that as a sign. His heart wanted Patrick, not Mark, he knew that now. Somehow, he needed to figure out a way to tell Patrick just what he was feeling and find out how Patrick felt about him.

CHAPTER
Six

JULIANNE walked to the table in her kitchen, where Patrick sat nursing a cup of coffee. "I think it's about time you tell me why you've been moping around my kitchen for the last three hours and have been a complete bear for two weeks," Julianne said as she pulled out a chair and sat down. Todd raced in, sliding to a stop in his sock feet, and Patrick lifted his cousin onto his lap. Julianne got up and then returned with a sippy cup that she set down in front of her son. "Here's your coffee," she told him, and Todd grabbed the cup and began to drink. It looked like apple juice to Patrick, and he smiled at his cousin's little deception. Julianne sat back down and pushed a pad in Patrick's direction. "Spill it. I know you've been hiding here during the day, and while I love the company and Todd adores having his uncle to play with, you haven't been your usual bubbly self."

Patrick scowled at her sarcasm, but he couldn't argue with her. As he sipped from his mug, he bounced his knee, and Todd giggled. Realizing he couldn't put it off any longer, he pulled the pad toward him. *"His old boyfriend came back,"* Patrick wrote.

"So," Julianne responded, pushing the pad back. "Old boyfriends show up like bad pennies."

"*I saw them kissing*," Patrick wrote, and he saw Julianne's eyes widen.

"Are you sure?"

Patrick nodded. "*I was having lunch with Ken and Hanna, and Mark*," Patrick scrawled the name as hastily as he could, as though it were a dirty word, "*showed up. He greeted Ken like an old friend, and I left because I didn't want to interfere and….*" Patrick paused. "*I went back and saw them kissing through the kitchen window.*" Patrick slid the pad back and hugged Todd to him.

"So they kissed. Are you sure it wasn't this Mark kissing Ken? You didn't hear what they were saying, did you?"

Patrick pushed back from the table, and Todd looked up at him. Patrick lifted the boy off his lap and handed him to Julianne. What he'd seen didn't take much of an explanation, and he'd been staying away for two weeks.

"So you got your heart broken," Julianne said as she took Todd. "It's not the end of the world, and he may not love you the way you wanted, but he's still your friend, and his daughter misses you, doesn't she?" Patrick looked at his shoes and nodded. "I understand about being hurt, but you avoiding that sick little girl is only making her wonder what she did wrong." Patrick lifted his gaze, and Julianne tilted her head slightly. "What?"

Patrick sat back down, and when Julianne settled Todd on her lap, he curled against her. "*They knocked on my door later that day, twice, and I hid from them.*" Patrick passed the note to Julianne, who simply shook her head.

"I don't know what to tell you. If he was kissing his ex, then he was. Have you seen this guy hanging around a lot?" Julianne inquired, and Patrick shook his head. He really hadn't, and as much as he'd tried to avoid Ken, he'd still kept an eye on him, and Mark's black Toyota hadn't been seen around their house.

"Then I have a piece of advice for you. Talk to him. Grab your best pad and pen and pay him a visit. Sit down face to face, pad to pad, and talk to him. If he isn't interested in you, then you'll know and can move on, but until you ask, you'll wonder. And continue to act"—Julianne smirked "a little creepy."

"*I wasn't spying on them or anything. It was an accident*," Patrick scrawled defensively.

"I know." Julianne reached out and patted his hand. "But you're obsessing over him, and that isn't good." Patrick had to agree with her. He knew he was preoccupied with Ken, but he couldn't help it. Maybe she was right and he needed to talk to him. The worst that could happen was Ken would tell him that he wasn't interested.

"You know all this insanity could be avoided if you just learned to communicate properly." Julianne lifted her mug and drank. "You're going to learn sign language. I'm going to sign you up for lessons, and we're all going to go, even Todd." Patrick began to shake his head, but Julianne stopped him with a stare. "You need to stop hiding and rejoin the rest of the world. At least think about it. The hospital has a program for the deaf, and they'll teach all of us sign language. If nothing else, you'll be able to communicate without having to write everything down."

Patrick nodded and sighed at the same time.

"Good. Now promise me you'll talk to Ken and find out where you stand." Julianne was determined. Patrick tried to look away, but she stared him down. Once again, he found himself agreeing. "Now finish your coffee and you can head on home. It's time for Todd's nap, and I can have a few hours to myself." Julianne set Todd on his feet, and he found some trucks and began playing on the floor. Patrick finished his coffee and said good-bye to his Todd before kissing Julianne on the cheek. Then he left and headed to his car for the nerve-racking drive home. He wasn't sure how he could confess to Ken how he felt, but he deserved to be told. And Patrick knew he deserved to know if Ken felt the same way. He couldn't seem to get the image of that kiss out of his head. It had hurt really badly to see Mark and Ken kissing, because he'd wished it was him. Patrick desperately wanted the person standing in front of Ken in his kitchen, holding those soft, smooth cheeks, and kissing Ken's full, red lips to be him. Was that too much to ask? After all he'd lost already, was finding someone to love him too much to hope for?

Patrick parked in front of his house and then walked the short distance to Ken's, shuffling up the walk as he tried to delay what he figured was the inevitable. Ken appeared to be home, and as he approached the front, Patrick knocked softly on the door and waited. It swung open, and Ken stood in the opening. Patrick smiled at the momentary delight in Ken's eyes, which dimmed a few seconds later. "I wasn't expecting to see you," Ken said, and Patrick nodded. His absence had obviously been missed. "Hanna has asked about you almost every day. She's worried about you," Ken told him in an accusing tone. Patrick knew that and he was sorry for it, but all he could do was nod and look down. He wasn't sure how Ken was going to react or if he was just going to close the door in his face. "Come in," Ken offered, and Patrick stepped inside.

Patrick looked around, but didn't see Hanna or any of the toys or paper that signified that she'd been around. He patted his chest, wondering if he'd brought a pad, but he hadn't.

"Hanna's taking a nap—she'll sleep for hours," Ken said softly. "She's been doing that more and more lately." Ken's lower lip trembled. "She started treatments again, but they're taking lot out of her." Ken looked devastated, and Patrick's heart felt squeezed in his chest. Without thinking, he stepped forward, tugging Ken into his arms. "She's not doing well, Patrick, and I don't know...." His thought trailed off in what sounded like a sob. "They say this is going to help her, but she keeps getting weaker and weaker."

There was nothing Patrick could do but hold Ken. He had no words of comfort, and instead he smoothed his hand over Ken's soft hair and lightly stroked his back. This was what he'd been dreaming of for weeks. He wasn't sure why Mark wasn't here to comfort Ken, but right now he didn't really care. He had Ken in his arms, and his head rested on Patrick's shoulders, his breath blowing on Patrick's skin. They stood there with the door still open for a while. Patrick was afraid to move, figuring Ken would remember who was holding him and need to step away. A light breeze blew across them, and Ken lifted his head off Patrick's shoulder, their eyes locking.

Ken's eyes seemed to hold all the magic of the world, as blue as the ocean and nearly as deep. His lips parted slightly, and Patrick leaned closer, swallowing hard. When Ken didn't pull back, Patrick moved closer yet, touching his lips to Ken's for the first time. The touch was so light, Patrick barely realized they'd begun to kiss until Ken leaned forward, deepening the touch.

Patrick didn't wait for an additional invitation. He cupped the back of Ken's head with his hand and deepened the kiss further. Ken moaned softly, and Patrick parted his lips, feeling Ken do the same. Patrick accepted the invitation, exploring Ken's mouth with his tongue. Ken continued making little noises in this throat that sounded as close to joyful music as anything Patrick had ever heard in his life. Lifting his leg, Patrick caught the door and kicked it closed, neither of them paying the slightest attention to the thud as the fresh breeze ceased. Not that Patrick noticed as he continuing pummeling Ken's mouth with kiss after kiss. He'd been dreaming of this for months. Ever since he'd first seen Ken, he'd wondered what his lips would taste like, and now he knew: sweet with a hint of spice.

Ken moaned again, and Patrick gentled the kiss before letting their lips part. Ken breathed deeply, like he'd just run a race, and Patrick stared into his eyes, wondering what Ken's reaction to his advance would be. He half expected to be told to leave, but instead Ken kissed him with a passion and need that curled Patrick's toes.

They moved together, kissing and holding each other as Ken guided him up the stairs. Patrick didn't look around as they moved, his entire attention focused on Ken. He hadn't come over expecting this, but when they reached Ken's bedroom, Patrick knew that if he got the chance to be with Ken just once, then he'd take it. Surging forward once Ken closed the door, Patrick kissed Ken all the way to the bed and then down onto the mattress. Ken groaned when Patrick slipped a hand beneath his shirt, and Patrick slid his hand over Ken's warm, smooth belly and chest. Ken's muscles ripped and shivered with what Patrick thought was excitement as he stroked upward, his fingers gliding over a nipple.

Ken vibrated beneath him, and Patrick shifted slightly, gripping the hem of Ken's shirt and lifting it up and over his head. Patrick stopped kissing just long enough to pull the fabric off and then resumed his attack on Ken's now kiss-swollen lips. Patrick broke the kiss and then tugged off his own shirt as Ken shimmied onto the bed, his half-lidded eyes glazed over with want. Patrick had never seen so sexy a sight in his life. Ken really wanted him, something Patrick had never thought he'd see. Prowling back onto the bed, Patrick straddled Ken's legs and hips, then stroked his hands up Ken's side and over his shoulders. He longed to tell Ken how beautiful he was, long and lean with pale skin that reminded Patrick of alabaster.

Patrick trailed his lips down Ken's neck and shoulder, listening as Ken gasped and moaned softly. At the base of his throat, Patrick found a spot that made Ken's entire body throb, and he licked and kissed that spot until Ken begged him to stop. Then he licked the spot again, and Ken's head rolled back and forth on the pillow as his salty-sweet flavor had Patrick's tongue tingling. Patrick loved the way he responded to him and the little noises Ken made as Patrick licked his way down his chest and belly, which nearly sent him into orbit. It had been a long time since he'd touched anyone like this. In fact, Patrick had figured after the accident that he'd never be able to touch someone like this again, but here he was with Ken, the man he'd been dreaming about for months.

"Do that again," Ken moaned softly as Patrick licked and sucked on one of his small, pink nipples, and he felt Ken arch into him when he did just that, sucking the hard little bud until he felt Ken writhe on the mattress beneath him.

Patrick kissed his way back to Ken's lips, pressing the other man's body against the mattress, feeling Ken's jeans-clad erection through his own pants. He felt Ken's hands work between them as his belt was opened and the fabric worked open; then Ken's hand slid down the back of his pants. Ken's other hand joined the first, and Patrick's breath hitched as Ken gripped and kneaded his butt. The intimate touch drove him wild, and Patrick ground his hips against Ken's as he did his best to work open Ken's pants. Ken pushed down his pants, and Patrick fumbled with Ken's, trying desperately to get them both naked. Eventually, Patrick realized his pants were hopelessly tangled around his legs, but he didn't give a damn as Ken rolled him in the bed, kissing him hard as he ground their hips together.

Ken slid his length along Patrick's, and he arched his back, gaping wide-mouthed in a silent cry as Ken moved against his cock. "You feel wonderful, Patrick," Ken whispered as he did it again, and then he stopped. "Have you been with anyone since…?"

Patrick shook his head. No one had touched him since the accident, not that he'd expected anyone would want to.

Ken sat up, staring into Patrick's eyes, his weight settling on Patrick's hips and legs, his cock jutting out from a nest of light brown curls. "You're beautiful, Patrick. You really are," Ken said as Patrick felt his gaze wander down his body. "You've kept yourself hidden away for a long time, haven't you?" Patrick nodded slowly, his eyes drinking in Ken's flawless skin. "Why? You're a special man with so much to give. Why would you keep it hidden away?" Ken leaned forward, lightly sucking Patrick's lips between his. "You're caring and thoughtful," Ken told him, punctuating each word with kisses that trailed further down Patrick's body. "I don't know what I would have done without you." Ken kissed the skin just above Patrick's belly button, and Patrick inhaled, sucking in his stomach as the kisses continued. "You're an amazing man, Patrick, and I care for you very much."

Patrick's cock throbbed as Ken kissed the skin just above the head. Holding his breath, Patrick willed Ken to touch him— just once was all he could ever want. Patrick clamped his eyes closed and grunted softly, as close to a gasp as he could come as Ken licked along his length and then took him into his mouth. Patrick's head throbbed, and he thrust his hips into the sensation. He felt Ken's hand on his hip, stilling him as Ken took him deeper. Patrick would have cried out as the wettest heat he'd ever felt in his life engulfed him, and in his head there was a litany of wonderful sounds, but all he could do was grunt softly and listen as Ken hummed slightly around him. Patrick cupped Ken's cheeks in his hands. His shaft slipped from Ken's mouth, and Ken crawled up Patrick's body, their lips meeting in a fierce kiss that had Patrick shaking and throbbing from head to toe. He wanted to tell Ken that he'd dreamed for months of being here like this with him, but all he could do was return the kisses with every ounce of the energy and passion that coursed through his body.

The kiss ended, and Patrick looked into Ken's eyes, a bit stunned by what he saw: lust, passion, and something he couldn't quite identify. He hoped it was what his heart had been wishing for, but his mind was a bit muddled, and then Ken shifted, sliding his lips down Patrick's shaft again, making everything except the ecstasy zinging through his body fly from his mind. Ken slid his mouth up and down his shaft, and Patrick had to keep himself from thrusting into the overwhelming sensation.

Then everything stopped. Ken stilled, and Patrick fisted the sheets in total frustration, his cock throbbing in Ken's mouth. He wanted to cry out and even opened his mouth. Slowly, Ken slid his lips up Patrick's shaft. Patrick slipped from Ken's lips and felt him kissing a trail up his skin. Ken kissed him hard, his body pressing onto Patrick's. Their shafts slid side by side, and Patrick cupped Ken's butt as their hips thrust. All of Patrick's control was stripped away. Holding Ken tightly, their body heat mingling, Patrick listened as Ken steadily and softly moaned into his ear. Patrick couldn't imagine that a more fitting accompaniment to lovemaking could possibly exist. Ken pressed his chest to Patrick's, their legs entwining as Patrick's pants finally slid off his legs and his cock slid against Ken's hot skin.

Patrick felt the pressure begin to build and he held tighter, thrusting harder as Ken did the same. Ken's breath hitched, and he groaned deeply. Then Patrick felt Ken's thrusts speed up, becoming erratic, and Patrick felt him still as liquid heat spread between them. Patrick smiled, clamped his eyes shut, and thrust hard as he tumbled over the edge, adding his own release to Ken's.

Patrick listened to Ken breathe as he caught his own breath, afraid to move and break the spell between them. He held Ken tight, letting their sweat and release mingle on his skin. Nothing in recent memory had felt so good. Touching Ken's cheeks,

Patrick brought Ken's face to his, kissing him softly with a slight smile.

Ken stilled, and Patrick did that same, both listening for a few seconds. Hearing nothing, Ken settled his head against Patrick's shoulder, and Ken continued holding him. "I need to get up soon," Ken explained. "I doubt she will, but Hanna could wake up, and I need to be there for her."

Patrick nodded and shifted on the bed. Ken sat up, and Patrick stood, searching the floor for his clothes. He should have known it would be like this, that once things were over, Ken would want him gone. He bent down and picked up his tangled underwear and pants and began straightening them out so he could put them on. "Patrick," Ken said softly, and he stood still when Ken touched his arm. "I don't want you to go." Patrick turned and stared into Ken's eyes, not understanding what he wanted. "I don't want Hanna to wake and find us like this, but I don't want you to go." Ken walked to his closet, his butt bobbing with each step. Getting out a robe, he put it on and turned back to Patrick. "I'll be right back after I check on Hanna." Ken left the room, and Patrick stood near the bed, still naked, wondering what he should do. He wanted to stay and see what Ken meant, but part of him said to run.

Then the door opened again and Ken walked in with a smile. "She's still asleep," Ken told him before moving closer. "And you're amazingly handsome," Ken added before tugging him into a kiss. "I think we need to talk, but after we clean up." Ken opened the bathroom door, and Patrick dropped the clothes he'd been holding onto the bed and followed Ken inside.

Ken turned on the water in the shower and took off his robe. Patrick didn't wait for an invitation before taking Ken in his arms, kissing him again as he rubbed their chests together. Patrick could already feel his body reacting once again, and Ken moaned softly into his kisses while Patrick stroked the soft skin of Ken's back and butt. The room began to fill with stream, and Patrick continued kissing Ken, not caring about anything other than having this man in his arms.

"Come with me," Ken said, and Patrick followed him into the shower. The near-scalding water tingled Patrick's skin, and Ken turned it down, letting the heat cascade over them both. "I've wanted you for a long time," Ken told him, and Patrick's eyes widened before he pointed to himself and then at Ken, nodding slowly. "You've felt the same way?" Ken asked, and Patrick nodded before pushing Ken against the tile, pressing his skin to Ken's as he attacked his mouth. Patrick might not have been able to speak, but he was bound and determined to take this opportunity to make sure Ken understood just how he felt.

By the time Patrick pulled back, Ken was breathing hard. Patrick smiled and reached for the bottle of soap. After filling his hands, he rubbed them together and then slowly smoothed them over Ken's chest. He watched as Ken rested his head back against the tile, and Patrick used the opportunity to explore. Ken's chest and stomach passed under his hands, muscles twitching, and Ken's breath hitched. There were so many things he wanted to ask, but instead he let his hands ask the questions, and Ken's body provided the answers. Ken's legs shook as he stroked below Ken's stomach and then along his thick length. Patrick lifted his gaze and met Ken's as he gripped and carefully stroked the thickening shaft. His eyes were nearly closed, his mouth slightly open, his breath coming in shallow pants. Patrick stroked hard, and Ken thrust his hips lightly to meet the movement. He wanted to be able to tell Ken all the things he was thinking, like how amazingly attractive he looked right now, and how hot it was that Ken could barely move because of the things Patrick was doing to him. Ken deserved to hear those things, but all Patrick could do was show him. Stepping closer, he pressed his chest to Ken's soapy skin, sliding them together, and very quickly he found his back pressed to the tile, with Ken grinning at him.

"For a man who can't speak, you're amazingly good at making your feelings known," Ken told him, and he felt Ken sucking on his neck. "So why don't I show you the same way." Ken moved away, and Patrick watched as he stepped back into the spray, the soap sluicing off his body. When Ken leaned back to wash his hair, Patrick let his eyes travel all along Ken's body, from glistening chest to narrow hips, jutting cock, and strong thighs. He also watched as Ken squeezed some soap on his hands and began washing Patrick's chest. He closed his eyes and let the sensation of being cared for wash over him.

When Ken slipped his hands to his hips and then along his cock, Patrick's breath hitched and he groaned deeply, or for him what approximated a groan. He opened his eyes and saw Ken smiling at him. Patrick hated most of the sounds he could make now—to him he sounded like an animal—but Ken seemed to like them, judging by the smile and by the way his grip tightened around Patrick's shaft. Patrick let his mouth fall open and his head fall backward as Ken knelt down in front of him, stroking Patrick's legs and thighs. Patrick's legs trembled, and he used the wall to keep himself upright as Ken's amazing hands slid between his legs, cupping his balls while a finger teased lightly at his opening. "I want you to come for me, Patrick. Show me how much you like what I'm doing to you," Ken told him. Ken moved his hand away from his balls, gripping his shaft tightly as he pulled and stroked, hard and fast. Patrick quickly lost control of his own body, giving himself over to Ken as the pressure quickly built inside his balls. He wanted to cry out, but nothing came. Every muscle in his body came alive all at once, and flashes of light moved behind Patrick's eyes as he came, quivering against the tile.

Patrick gasped for breath and did his best to stop his legs from buckling. Once he'd caught his breath, he pulled Ken to him. "I came when you did," Ken told him, and Patrick gentled his touch as Ken guided them beneath the water. They stood together until the water began to cool. Ken turned it off and stepped out, handing Patrick a towel, and once they were dry, they went back onto Ken's bedroom to dress before Ken led him downstairs.

"I need to check on Hanna, and then you and I can talk," Ken said, and Patrick sat and waited, listening to Ken's footsteps.

Patrick shifted nervously, sitting on the edge of the chair as he waited for Ken to come back downstairs. Eventually he heard light footsteps, and then Ken walked back into the room and sat down across from him. "Just a minute," he said before getting up again. Ken wasn't gone long, and when he returned, he had a pad and pen that he set on the coffee table.

Patrick picked it up. "*How is Hanna?*" he wrote quickly.

"She's still asleep," Ken answered, and Patrick nodded, locking his eyes on Ken's, hoping for a little more information. "I'm not sure how to describe it. The doctors say they're hopeful she'll improve, but every treatment leaves her weaker than the last one. I suppose I should be grateful she isn't in the hospital, but it seems like all she does is sleep. That's probably good for her, because it gives her body a chance to heal, but I long to hear her laugh and play again. I just don't know if she ever will." Ken's voice trembled, and Patrick shifted so he was sitting next to him on the sofa and reached for Ken's hand. The thought of anything happening to that little girl made Patrick's heart ache, and he wished he could do something to help. "Patrick, I'm not sure how much more she's going to be able to take."

Patrick nodded softly, feeling Ken's worry and anxiety like a body blow. Letting go of Ken's hand, Patrick reached for the pad. "*Is there anything I can do to help?*"

"Pray," Ken answered softly. "I believe that's all any of us can do." Ken took a deep breath and held it, closing his eyes, and Patrick saw a tear run down Ken's face. "She told me last week that she wants to be Barbie for Halloween. I didn't understand why she was telling me that when it's barely summer, but I'm starting to think she's beginning to realize she won't make it till then."

"I'll see if I can find her the costume," Patrick wrote, his hands shaking. This wasn't the conversation he'd been expecting to have when Ken had said they needed to talk, but this was much more important.

"Thank you. Halloween or not, she'll love it," Ken said; then he swallowed hard.

Patrick looked around the room and saw a box of tissues on one of the end table. He got up, retrieved it, and then set the box on the coffee table before looking for the pad again, but he didn't know how to write the question that had kept running through his mind. Was now even the right time to ask? Patrick figured it wasn't, and he left the pad where it was and simply tugged Ken into a hug that lasted until Ken reached for a tissue.

"We do need to talk about what happened," Ken said as he wiped his eyes. Patrick nodded and waited for Ken to continue, figuring it was probably easiest for him to say what he needed to. "I care for you, Patrick, I do. You're a sweet man, and anyone would be lucky to have you in their life."

Patrick tilted his head slightly in confusion. *"I understand. You still have feelings for that Mark guy,"* Patrick wrote and passed the pad to Ken.

"I do, but not those kinds of feelings. Not anymore," Ken explained, and Patrick narrowed his eyes. "He came back a few weeks ago and told me he wanted me back, but Mark isn't the person I want in my life." Ken took Patrick's hands in his. "There are so many unknowns in our lives right now." Ken turned toward the stairs, and Patrick nodded, knowing what Ken meant. "I'm not sure there's room for anyone."

Patrick turned away, unprepared for how much those words hurt. He turned to look out the window so Ken couldn't see the disappointment he was sure was written all over his face. It seemed that Ken did like him, and while Patrick didn't understand the whole kiss thing he'd seen between Ken and Mark, he believed what Ken told him.

"Patrick," Ken said, and he turned his head back to Ken once again, schooling his expression as best he could. "I'm talking about you. I like you very much." Ken pulled one of his hands away. "You have a kind heart, and I'd never want to hurt you. But you deserve better than what I can give you. Hanna is going to take all my energy, and I'm not sure how much I'm going to have to give to anyone."

"*Do you want me to go?*" Patrick scrawled nervously on the pad after tearing off the old sheet.

"No. I don't want you to leave. I really want you to stay, but I don't know how fair I'm being to you." Ken shifted on the sofa. "You don't deserve to be put aside or to have to wait until Hanna…." Ken's voice broke, and Patrick tightened his hold on Ken's hands for a few seconds before reluctantly breaking contact to pick up the pad once more.

"*You don't think I understand? I know what fear feels like. I know….*" The thoughts and emotions ran over themselves and seemed to get lost as Patrick tried to write. All his feelings got jumbled up on their way to the paper and all that ended up on the pad was gibberish. Taking a deep breath, Patrick flipped the page and began again. "*I know what it feels like to lose something special. My gift was taken away with the accident, and you're afraid that your gift is going to be taken from you,*" Patrick wrote as Ken peered over his shoulder. Turning his head, Patrick saw Ken nod. "*I feel the same way about you, and it would be a shame to throw away that gift.*" Patrick hoped he was making sense, because his mind was running in a million different directions.

Giving up, Patrick tossed the pad onto the table and turned toward Ken, locking their gazes. Patrick cupped Ken's cheeks and kissed him with everything he had.

At first Ken seemed shocked, and his lips didn't move, but Patrick had to convey what he was feeling, so he threw himself into the kiss as though it were the only lifeline keeping him from falling into the abyss. Shifting his weight, Patrick pressed Ken backward. He felt Ken's arms wind around his back, and then Ken returned the kisses, moaning softly under Patrick's onslaught. Ken's lips parted, and Patrick surged his tongue between them, getting a full dose of Ken's heady, sweet flavor. Patrick's body reacted with gusto, regardless of the fact that he'd come twice less than an hour before. Patrick pushed the physical desire aside, concentrating instead on conveying just what he felt to Ken. *He has to know, I have to make him understand.*

When Patrick was afraid he was about to pass out from lack of oxygen, he broke the kiss with a gasp for air. Ken seemed to do the same, staring up at him with wide-eyed surprise. Patrick had leaned forward, ready to attack Ken's luscious lips once again, when he heard movement from upstairs. Ken froze, and Patrick did the same. Footsteps sounded on the stairs, and Patrick slipped off the sofa, extending his hand so Ken could get up. He couldn't help smiling at Ken's swollen, just-kissed lips. Let Ken think about that for a while.

"Daddy," Hanna said, and Ken left the room. Patrick checked that he was presentable and sat on the sofa as Ken came in the room, carrying Hanna in his arms. He had to look away for a second so he could remove the shocked expression from his face. Over the past few weeks, Hanna had lost weight. Her face was thinner and her eyes a bit hollow-looking. Ken set her on the sofa next to him, and Patrick leaned down, getting a hug and kiss. "I missed you, Mr. Patrick," Hanna told him, and Patrick immediately regretted staying away. If Ken hadn't told him how

Hanna was doing, he could have seen it in her and the way she leaned against him. It almost made him wonder if this was the same girl he'd seen a few weeks earlier picking flowers out in the yard.

"He missed you too," Ken responded for him, and Patrick nodded and smiled slightly. "Are you hungry?"

"Can I have mac-cheese?" Hanna asked, looking up at him, and Patrick nodded slowly before glancing at Ken, who seemed to understand what he needed and handed him the pad from the table.

"*I need to get the ingredients*," Patrick wrote.

"We still have your dish," Ken told him.

"I'll get what I need and come back," Patrick wrote before giving Hanna a kiss on the forehead. Slowly he got up off the sofa, giving Hanna a chance to shift next to her dad.

"Thank you, Patrick," Ken told him, and Patrick leaned down, kissing Ken lightly. When he stepped back, he glanced at Hanna and saw her smile. Then he left the house.

Inside his home, Patrick checked the cupboards and made a list of what he needed before leaving the house again, heading to the small grocery store in town. Pushing the cart up the aisle, Ken picked the cheese and macaroni he needed, along with some ice cream, before heading to the checkout. The ladies he passed said hello, and Patrick smiled and nodded at each of them. The checkout lady talked to him the whole time he was in line, and Patrick smiled as he bagged his groceries and paid for them.

"See you soon," she said as Patrick lifted the bag with his purchases, and he again nodded and smiled before hurrying out to his car. By the time he arrived back at Ken's, Patrick had nodded and smiled to the point he thought his head would fall off. He got out of the car and carried the bag of ingredients to the door and knocked. To his surprise, Hanna opened the door.

"Is that for mac-cheese?" she asked, and Patrick nodded, stepping inside. "Can I help?" she asked as she closed the door and followed Patrick into the kitchen. He looked around, but didn't see Ken right away, but then he wandered in from the back of the house, along with the smell of paint. Patrick set the bag on the counter and put the ice cream in the freezer. Then he brought over one of the kitchen chairs for Hanna to stand on.

"Is Patrick showing you how to cook?" Ken asked, and Hanna nodded and grinned.

"I'm gonna help," she said, and Ken leaned with his butt against the edge of the counter, wiping his hands on a rag. "That's stinky," Hanna said, pointing at Ken's rag and then holding her nose.

"Okay," Ken agreed and left the kitchen, returning a few seconds later without the rag, and then washed his hands again. Ken brought the casserole dish to the counter, and they got to work. His mother's recipe for macaroni and cheese wasn't difficult, and Patrick helped Hanna grate the cheese. After he cooked the macaroni, they put together the casserole. Patrick couldn't explain what he was doing, but he showed Hanna how he made the dish, and once it was together, he turned on the oven and placed the dish inside. After closing the oven door, Patrick set the timer. "Hanna, why don't you set the table?" Ken asked.

Hanna gingerly climbed down from the chair and slowly moved around the kitchen before bringing the silverware to the table. Ken helped her, getting the plates and glasses for her and setting them on the table. When the chore was done, Hanna quietly went back into the living room, and Patrick heard the television turn on. "She'll be asleep in less than ten minutes,"

Ken told him. "That little amount of activity will have worn her out."

Patrick didn't know what to say and followed Ken into the living room, where Hanna rested on the sofa, her eyes already half closed. Ken covered her with a blanket, and Hanna stirred. "I promise we'll get you when the mac-cheese is ready," Ken whispered before kissing her forehead, and Hanna settled under the blanket, already curling up to go to sleep.

Patrick reached for the pad that was still resting on the coffee table. "*Sorry. I didn't mean to wear her out,*" he wrote, and Ken shook his head,

"You didn't," he said, moving out of the room. "She got to have a bit of fun with you. She would have tired just as fast if she had been sitting at the table drawing pictures." Ken stood in the doorway, watching Hanna sleep, and Patrick rested his chin on Ken's shoulder, wishing more than anything in the world that she would be okay. If there was any chance in the world that he'd ever be able to talk and sing again, Patrick knew he'd trade that chance to make Hanna better. After setting the pad on the hall table, Patrick wound his arms around Ken's waist and lightly kissed the back of his neck. Patrick's heart was being torn in two as he watched Hanna sleep.

Helpless. That was only word that came to mind to describe how Patrick felt. He knew Ken felt the same way, and there was nothing for either of them to do. Eventually Patrick stepped away and followed Ken into the kitchen, picking up the pad as he went. They sat silently at the table, each lost in his thoughts. Patrick jumped slightly when the oven timer sounded, and he stood up, checking the casserole before turning off the oven and pulling the dish out, setting it on one of the stove burners to cool a little bit.

"I'll wake Hanna in a little while," Ken said softly, and Patrick nodded as the scent of the food filled the room. "Don't be surprised if she doesn't eat much," Ken warned and then went quiet. He didn't seem in the mood to talk, so they just sat. After about twenty minutes, Ken left the room. He returned with Hanna draped over his chest, her head resting on his shoulder. "Your mac-cheese is ready," Ken said before setting her into her chair. Hanna blinked a few times and yawned as Patrick dished up some dinner for each of them.

Ken poured glasses of milk, and they ate. Patrick noticed that both he and Ken watched every bite Hanna took. "This is good," she said. Patrick hadn't given her much, and she ate what was on her plate. She handed her plate to Patrick, and he gave her a bit more. She ate part of the second helping and drank some more of her milk before it became obvious that she was done.

Hanna sat with them while they finished eating, picking and eating a little bit more. Once they were done, Ken helped her down. "Why don't you draw a thank-you picture for Patrick?" Ken asked.

"Okay," Hanna said, and she slowly left the room.

"Sometimes I can see the Hanna I remember come through," Ken said as he stared after Hanna. After a few minutes, Ken left the room. Patrick cleaned up the dishes, placing them in the sink before joining the others.

Hanna had indeed drawn a number of pictures, one of which was given to him with a grin that nearly broke Patrick's heart. Patrick hugged her good-bye. "Will I see you tomorrow?" she asked.

Patrick nodded and crossed his heart with his hands. Then he hugged Ken, kissing him lightly before walking to the door. They both said good-bye, and Patrick waved before walking outside in the evening air, pulling the door closed behind him. At first he started for home, but kept on walking to the corner and then around the block. When he got back to his house, Patrick hurried inside and sat at the kitchen table, where he composed a note that said everything he wanted. Pulling the page off the pad, he folded it and tucked it into a pocket before leaving again and driving to Julianne's.

He knocked, and Julianne's husband, George, opened the door. "Patrick," he said happily, shaking hands with him before stepping aside so he could enter.

Todd raced through the house, calling "Uncle Patwick," and Patrick scooped him off his feet to giggles and laughter. "Mama, Uncle Patwick is here."

"I see that," Julianne said as she came out of the kitchen. "We were just about to eat. Are you hungry?" Patrick shook his head and pulled out the paper from his pocket, handing it to Julianne. George looked over her shoulder. Julianne moved away, and he moved with her, so she read it out loud.

"*I need your help. Hanna isn't doing well, and Ken isn't sure she's going to make it through the end of the year. Even Hanna seems to be looking just around the corner,*" Julianne read, and Patrick saw her wipe her eyes. "*She wants to be a Barbie Ballerina for Halloween and I promised Ken I would try to find her the costume. I know you can sew. Do you think you could make her the costume?*" Patrick was happy he'd taken the time to write this before he'd come over because he wouldn't be able to now. He met Julianne's gaze and saw her nod.

"Of course I'll make the costume for her. I think I have a pattern that will work," Julianne said before turning back to the letter.

"*I was thinking that maybe we could arrange to have a Halloween party of sorts at their house. I have some decorations at the house and I was hoping you'd help me. Maybe Todd, you, and George could dress up in costumes, too, and the kids could trick-or-treat at my house and Ken's. I know it would be small,*

129

but it would give Hanna a chance to have some fun," Patrick had written. "*She gets so tired so quickly that we can't go very far, but I'd like to give her what I can.*" Patrick had sort of run out of words at this point in his note, and he looked at George and Julianne.

"Does Ken know how you feel about him? I know you care for Hanna, but you're also doing this because of how you feel about Ken," Julianne said, and Patrick nodded before reaching for the paper.

"*Yes, I think so. We talked today,*" Patrick wrote, and Julianne read his note. He felt her looking him over and his cheeks warmed under her gaze. Patrick knew the minute Julianne realized what had happened, but to her credit, she kept quiet… for now. Patrick knew when they were alone he'd be pressed for details.

"I just have one question for you," Julianne asked as she handed Patrick back the piece of paper, looking at George, who nodded. "When do you want to do this?"

CHAPTER *Seven*

KEN arrived at Dr. Pierson's office with Hanna. After getting her out of the car, he held her hand as they walked into the medical office building near the hospital in Marquette. Patrick had offered to come along, but Ken had explained that this was just a checkup and that Hanna wasn't having a treatment this week, which Ken was grateful for. For the last three weeks or so, Patrick had done a lot of the cooking for them and had sort of stepped into their lives. Hanna was eating again, and she seemed to be getting a little stronger. Ken had no illusions that once treatments started again, she'd become weaker, but hope seemed to be lifting for them.

"Will Patrick be there when we get home?" Hanna asked as they walked into the elevator.

"He'll probably be over to see you shortly after you get home," Ken told her, hoping that he'd be over, not just for Hanna but for him, as well. They'd been spending time together, just the two of them, and Ken found he relished those times, even if they were often short and farther apart than he would have liked.

"Are they going to poke me?" Hanna asked, pulling Ken out of his thoughts.

"I'm sorry, sweetheart, they probably are," Ken answered. With each appointment, they usually took blood so they could measure her progress.

Hanna patted his hand lightly. "It's okay, Daddy. I'm used to it." Hanna turned as the door opened, and Ken felt an almost debilitating sense of anger wash over him. No child should ever get used to having needles poked into them. Ken wanted to scream at how unfair it all was. Hanna had been through hell and there was still more to go. "Daddy," Hanna said, tugging him toward the open elevator doors.

Ken cleared his mind and followed Hanna through the familiar hallways to the doctor's office. By the time they pushed open the door to Dr. Pierson's waiting room, Ken had let go of most of his anger. He knew it wasn't anyone's fault. It was just that whenever Hanna hurt, he hurt too. "Morning, Hanna," the receptionist said from behind the counter. "Dr. Pierson will be with you in just a minute."

"Thank you," Hanna said and sat down in one of the chairs, picking up one of the books. They'd been here so many times that they both had a routine. Hanna looked at the pictures in the books, and Ken sat next to her, thumbing nervously through a magazine without actually seeing the pages. A few minutes later, the nurse, Shirley, called them back, and they walked down the now-familiar hallway to the examination room, stopping at the scale along the way.

"I need a blood sample," Shirley said, and Hanna held up her arm, the way she did for every appointment now. Ken's heart lurched at the resigned look on Hanna's face.

No six-year-old should ever look like that, Ken thought as Shirley talked to Hanna all through the process.

"You're one of my best patients ever," Shirley said when she was done, and she reached into her pocket, then handed

Hanna a red lollipop. Hanna took it with a small smile before giving the nurse a hug and telling her thank you. "The doctor should be just a minute," Shirley said before patting Ken on the shoulder and then leaving the room.

Hanna sat on the edge of the examination table, her feet swinging slowly back and forth. Ken knew he was a lot more nervous and upset than Hanna was.

The door opened a few minutes later, and Dr. Pierson came in. Hanna slid off the table and walked to Dr. Pierson, giving her a hug that was returned carefully, but caringly, by the doctor. "You seem better," Dr. Pierson said as she lifted Hanna up onto the examination table. "Let's have a look at you."

Ken helped Hanna lift off her shirt, and then he held it for her while the doctor examined Hanna's chest, listened to her lungs, and then carefully examined her arms, legs, and the port. She looked in Hanna's ears, eyes, throat, and nose. "Does anything hurt?" she asked as she had Hanna lie back so she could thump things.

"Sometimes my head," Hanna told her, and Dr. Pierson nodded.

"You appear to have a little more energy."

"She's also eating more," Ken supplied. He knew that was largely due to Patrick making Hanna's favorite foods every chance he got.

"Mr. Patrick makes the best mac-cheese and chicken nuggets. Daddy burns 'em," Hanna supplied with a giggle. She knew she was tattling.

"Whatever you're doing, keep it up. She's gained a pound or so, and that's very good," the doctor said as she finished up. Hanna sat back up, and Ken helped her put her shirt back on.

"You're doing well, and depending on the results of your blood work, I'd like to perform another treatment next week."

Ken lifted Hanna down, setting her on her feet. "So soon? She's been doing so well."

"I know. But if we wait too long, we'll be back where we started." The doctor looked as concerned as Ken felt. "I'll call you tomorrow, and we can discuss what we need to do." Ken nodded and lifted Hanna into his arms. He knew this was what had to be done, but he hated the thought of Hanna losing what little energy she had all over again. "I know this is hard, but it's the best choice for getting her better," the doctor added.

Ken knew she was right. "I know."

"Make sure she gets plenty of rest, and let her spend as much time as she can outdoors. The fresh air will be good for her."

"I will," Ken said, walking toward the door. He thanked the doctor once again before checking out at the desk and then heading out to the car. Hanna was quiet most of the way home, but as they turned on their street, Ken heard her gasp. When he parked in front of the house, he saw pumpkins sitting on either side of the front door and paper ghosts hanging on the porch. Spiderwebs covered some of the bushes, and what looked like a small group of children wandered along the sidewalk between his house and Patrick's in what looked like Halloween costumes. Ken got out and helped an excited Hanna out of her seat. She hurried to the front door to look at the decorations.

"Happy Halloween," a woman in a witch costume told him, and Ken recognized her as Patrick's cousin. "We're having an early Halloween party. Would you and Hanna like to join us?" she asked, and Hanna hurried over. "I have a costume for you," she said to Hanna, and Ken stared at her in surprise and disbelief. He knew his mouth was hanging open as he followed her down the street to Patrick's. His house was even more decorated than theirs, with a table on the side lawn covered with a Halloween tablecloth and pumpkin party favors. Ken could feel Hanna's excitement, and he watched her look all around. "Would you like to get into costume too?" Julianne asked as she knelt down in front of Hanna. She looked up at Ken, and he nodded. Hanna then let herself be led away into Patrick's house, and Ken followed.

Inside, he found Patrick in the kitchen making up what looked like plates of cookies shaped like pumpkins and witches. Patrick smiled at him and handed him two trays. Figuring he'd been put to work, Ken carried them outside and placed them on the table beneath the huge trees that shaded Patrick's yard. The kids were playing some sort of game, yelling and laughing. Adults, most in costume, sat in lawn chairs, watching and talking. Ken took a seat and introductions were made. Most of the people were friends of Julianne's, and the children were friends of Todd's, but they all seemed nice.

"Daddy, look!" Hanna cried as she walked across the grass, holding Patrick's hand. The smile on her face rivaled the sun, and Ken couldn't help noticing the proud look on Patrick's face. "I'm Ballerina Barbie," Hanna said as she did a slow spin.

"You look beautiful, sweetheart," Ken said, feeling a little choked up.

"Can I play with the kids?" Hanna asked as she longingly looked over at them.

"Yes, but take it easy and don't get too tired." Ken hated that he had to say that to a six-year-old. She should be able to run and play to her heart's content.

"I promise," she said, and she walked to where the other kids were playing. Ken couldn't help thinking that she should be running and laughing, not worried about getting tired and falling down.

"It's okay," the woman sitting next to him, who'd introduced herself as Alice, told him. "We're all here, and we'll help watch out for her." She looked back at the children, and Ken followed her gaze. Hanna held hands with one of the other little girls, also dressed as a Barbie, who carried a pink case, and they walked away to a spot under one of the trees. "That's my daughter Mary," Alice told Ken. "She and your Hanna will probably play dolls for hours." Sure enough, the case was opened, and the two girls sat down together.

"It's been awhile since she was able to do something normal like this," Ken commented as he watched them for a while.

"I understand you're a famous artist," Alice said, and Ken nodded. He'd long ago stopped denying his success. "What are you working on now?"

Ken pulled his gaze away from Hanna. "A series of portraits. I haven't been able to work much in the last year or so, but mostly I've been painting Hanna. Some are the way she looked before she was sick and some are pictures of the way she looks now." He wasn't about to tell anyone about the paintings he'd done of Patrick. Those were too personal, and he wasn't ready to let them go. He wasn't even sure he could let Patrick see them even, at least not yet. "But I don't have much time to work, much to my agent's complete dismay." Ken shrugged. He had more than enough money, and Hanna needed him right now. That was all that really mattered.

"I'd love to see your work sometime," Alice said a bit flirtatiously, and Ken smiled. He saw Patrick walking across the yard, carrying a few more trays. He looked amazingly happy, and he set down the trays before watching Hanna play. Then his gaze shifted to Ken, who felt it like a brand on his skin, and he shifted in his chair. Ken motioned Patrick over and stood up, kissing Patrick lightly.

"Thank you. This was just what Hanna needed," Ken told him, and Patrick nodded before blushing bright red. Ken couldn't help smiling as Patrick made a hasty retreat back toward the house.

Without turning around, Ken knew that every adult eye was on him at that moment. He schooled the devious smile off his face and turned around as everyone tried to look nonchalant. Ken had found out a long time ago that there was nothing like a little dose of reality to cool the thoughts of any woman with illusions that she had even the slightest chance to ever be Mrs. Brighton. Sitting back down, he turned to Alice. "I'm sorry for the interruption. I'd be happy to show you some of my work sometime." Alice's interest had definitely waned.

"Who wants to bob for apples?" Julianne called, and the kids gathered around a tub in the yard. Ken hurried home to get his camera, returning as Hanna took her turn. She didn't get an apple, but Ken got great pictures of her trying. The next little boy dunked his head in the tub and came up with an apple, water running all down him. Everyone cheered, and the little show-off actually bowed.

The afternoon continued with more games for the kids, and then the dinner was brought out. Most of the kids sat at the table, with the adults on lawn chairs. After they ate, there was a scavenger hunt for the kids, which was a huge hit. As evening came on, each child was given a small bag and each adult a small bowl of candy. They positioned themselves all around the yard and the kids "trick-or-treated" the adults. By the time that was over, Hanna was leaning against Ken, and he lifted her onto his lap.

"Maybe she and Mary can get together to play sometime," Alice offered from the chair next to him.

"I think Hanna would like that," Ken answered. He wasn't too sure how much playing Hanna would be up for once the treatments started again, but having a friend would be good for her. "I'll give you our number before you leave."

Hanna fell asleep in Ken's arms, still clutching her bag of loot. As twilight approached, people began to head home, and Ken stood up, still holding a sleeping Hanna. "Is it time to take her home?" Julianne asked, now in regular clothes.

"Yes. She's been asleep for some time now," Ken said, and then his voice failed him. This had been just what both of them needed. "Thank you so much for including us in your fun." A young boy careened into her legs, and she lifted him into her arms.

"You're very welcome," she said before turning to her son. "Say good night, Todd."

"Night," he cried with a grin, and Ken caught Patrick's eye before walking the short distance home. The pumpkins on his porch, that he now knew were plastic, had been lit, and he wanted to wake Hanna so she could see them, but instead he carried her inside. Hanna barely woke up as Ken got her out of the costume. Once he had Hanna in bed, Ken kissed her forehead and quietly left the room. He took the costume with him, folding it carefully so he could return it. As he came downstairs, he heard footsteps on the porch and then a soft knock at the door.

Patrick opened the door, holding a plate of cookies, and joined Ken on his porch. "Are these for Hanna?" Ken asked, and Patrick nodded. "She was so tired she barely woke up at all when I put her to bed." Patrick stepped inside, and Ken took the plate of cookies. "She had the best time," Ken told Patrick. "Your cousin is something else," he added as he walked back toward the kitchen, with Patrick following behind him. "I set the costume aside so you could take it back to her."

Patrick shook his head, motioning upward. "Are you saying that was for Hanna?" Ken asked, and Patrick nodded. "But it was handmade." Patrick stepped closer. "Did you have that made for Hanna?" Ken asked, and Patrick nodded slowly and moved still closer. Ken set the plate on the counter. "You have to give me Julianne's address so we can send her a thank-you note," Ken added. He'd give anything to be able to unlock some of the mysteries that lurked within this generously giving man. But those thoughts zipped away as Patrick drew him close. Ken tilted his chin upward, and Patrick held him tight before kissing him hard as he pressed him back against the counter. Ken had been with Mark for two years, and he'd never made him so totally weak in the knees from just a kiss. Patrick pressed for entrance with his tongue, and Ken threw his arms around Patrick's neck and held on as his senses were overwhelmed by all things Patrick.

His scent drove Ken wild, and he gripped Patrick more tightly as the delicious attack on his lips continued to build. Ken thought for a few seconds that Patrick's intention was to press him onto the counter, but then the kiss softened and ended. Ken sucked in air quickly, locking his gaze with Patrick's deep, almost hypnotic eyes. Ken parted his lips to say something, but Patrick kissed the words, and the thought, away.

When the kiss ended again, Ken's chest was heaving and his lungs craved oxygen, but still he didn't want the kiss to end. His life seemed in a constant state of turmoil, but in Patrick's arms that receded, at least for a while. Patrick moved away from him, and Ken groaned softly until he felt Patrick take his hand, leading him out of the kitchen, turning off the lights as they moved through the house. As they climbed the stairs, the only sound was their footsteps and the slight creak of the steps. Patrick led him to Hanna's door, and Ken peered inside at her sleeping form in the bed. She rolled over in her sleep while he watched, and then seemed to settle once more. Ken looked at Patrick, and he guided them toward Ken's bedroom. The hall light flicked out with a soft click, and Patrick urged him forward in near darkness.

The bedroom door closed, and Ken stood still, waiting for whatever Patrick had in mind. Ken heard Patrick's soft breathing and felt his heat as he approached. In the darkness, he felt Patrick grip his shirt, lifting it up his body. Ken raised his arms, and Patrick pulled off the shirt. Ken waited once again. As his eyes adjusted, he saw Patrick tug off his own shirt and drop it to the floor. Patrick reached for him, holding him as he moved closer. Their chests touched, and Patrick stroked along his back as he dipped his head to the base of Ken's neck.

Ken jumped slightly as Patrick licked and kissed along his shoulder, his lips and tongue leaving a trail of damp coolness on his warm skin. Arching his neck, he moaned softly as Patrick licked the base of his neck before continuing up along his throat. Each movement seemed so deliberately languid and slow that Ken couldn't help rolling his head back, letting Patrick have his way with him.

Patrick's lips found his in the dark, the kiss, like the touch, soft and slow, meant to tease and let the excitement build. Ken lifted his head to meet Patrick's gaze and began moving toward the bed, but Patrick held him still, kissing hard, telling him that he was in charge.

Excitement zinged through Ken at the thought of giving their pleasure over to Patrick. He had to be strong all the time for Hanna, and Patrick had just signaled that he didn't have to be strong right now, that Patrick would take care of him—and Ken wanted to be taken care of. Ken groaned loudly when Patrick's lips tugged on his as they slipped away.

Patrick's heat slipped away, and Ken stood still... waiting, until Patrick stroked his hands over his chest and slowly down his stomach. Ken held his breath as he felt Patrick pause above his belt. His pants had felt one size too tight for awhile, and he sucked in his breath further, hoping against hope that Patrick would follow the trail. He did. Patrick teased at the waistband of his briefs before sliding further. Ken gasped when Patrick brushed against his straining cock, wishing for more. But Patrick seemed content to take his time, and Ken wanted to scream at the near agonizing pace of Patrick's seduction. Ken knew that was exactly what Patrick was doing, and he also knew that he could beg until he was blue in the face. Patrick would take care of him in his own time, and Ken would let him.

Ken felt Patrick open his belt, his hand gliding back from inside his briefs. Then his belt was tugged off, and Ken heard it chink on the floor. Ken's pants were opened next, then pushed past his hips to pool around his ankles. He stepped out of them and stood naked and as excited as possible in front of Patrick, who guided him back onto the bed. Climbing onto the mattress, Ken watched as Patrick removed his own pants, letting them fall to the floor. He was just as aroused as Ken, who watched as Patrick prowled toward the bed, his cock swinging with each step. He moaned softly when Patrick's weight descended on his body, Patrick's warm smooth skin sliding along his. This was definitely heaven, and as Patrick rubbed his cock along his, Ken's head began to swim. He bucked slowly, and Patrick touched his hip lightly to still him, then kissed him once again before sliding down his body.

Patrick kissed a line down his chest as he caressed Ken's skin, sucking lightly on a nipple before driving him crazy with the circular motion of his tongue. Before he'd met Patrick, Ken would have thought it strange for sex to be nearly completely silent, but Patrick compensated for his lack of vocality with his hands and tongue, letting them speak louder than the mightiest shout. He himself was usually a very vocal lover, but Ken didn't feel the need to speak either. Instead, he let his hands wander over

Patrick's back and shoulders, using his own hands to express the care and passion he felt for Patrick.

Ken arched his back as Patrick slithered further down his body, licking the skin beneath his belly button. The anticipation was killing him, and Ken fisted the sheets as Patrick stroked Ken's cock with his chest, sliding his entire torso over his throbbing erection. "Patrick," Ken cried out, unable to keep it inside.

That seemed to please Patrick, and he did it again before dipping his head and taking Ken's cock between his lips. Ken could barely breathe as he was taken deeper and deeper into Patrick's searing hot mouth. He tried not to move his hips, but failed miserably as the desire built from deep inside him. Patrick took him deep and hard, tickling the skin above Ken's cock with his nose. "Jesus," Ken swore, clamping his eyes closed as he yanked at the covers on the bed. Patrick bobbed his head, alternately sliding his lips up Ken's shaft and then sucking him deep once again. Ken released the covers, carding his fingers through Patrick's soft hair. He didn't want to overwhelm him, but the need to move was so great he couldn't control it. Ken slowly thrust his hips, and Patrick sucked harder.

Ken could already feel the tingling starting, signaling that he was getting close. His thrusts became a little ragged, and Patrick lifted his head away. Ken growled deeply at the loss, and he felt Patrick soothingly stroke along his chest. There were times when he wished Patrick could tell him what he had in mind, and this was definitely one of those times. However, Ken found out pretty quickly when Patrick rolled him onto his stomach. Ken felt Patrick's weight on his legs. The bed shifted, and then Patrick kissed his shoulders and across his back before licking a line down his spine. Ken kept expecting Patrick to stop, but he didn't. The weight shifted again, and Ken felt Patrick caress his butt, fingers kneading his cheeks, lips kissing and licking the skin. Ken thought he was going to die, but when Patrick parted his cheeks, licking down his cleft, Ken was transported, and he knew he was in heaven.

Patrick parted his cheeks with his thumbs, teasing Ken's opening with agonizingly wonderful friction. Ken pressed back and gasped when one of Patrick's thumbs teased the skin around his entrance. "Oh, God," Ken moaned softly, though he felt Patrick's thumb move away, and then, God almighty, if it wasn't replaced by Patrick's tongue. Patrick seemed to know exactly what to do to make Ken feel like his head was ready to explode. Fingers, tongue—all of it combined was driving him crazy. He turned his head to see what Patrick was doing even as Patrick caressed his inner thighs, and Ken spread his legs further, opening himself wide for as much of Patrick's tongue magic as he could get.

How Patrick could play his body like an instrument, Ken had no idea, but Patrick had successfully stopped every thought but those surrounding what he was doing. It felt like Patrick was intent on single-handedly rimming Ken into absolute oblivion, and if he kept this up much longer, Ken expected his brain to totally overload. Maybe that was Patrick's intention? Reaching to the head of the bed, Ken grabbed a pillow, and after wedging it beneath his head, he grabbed it in his fists and held tight as Patrick took him on what seemed like the ride of his life. All he could do was whimper and moan constantly as Patrick tongue-fucked him within an inch of his life.

"Patrick," Ken whined softly. "Fuck me before I die." He quivered from head to toe, rocking back and forth on his knees. His legs felt as though they would give out at any minute, and his cock throbbed and slapped against his belly.

Patrick breached him with a finger, sliding it into his body, and Ken sighed at the welcome intrusion. When Patrick crooked his finger slightly, Ken's legs collapsed from under him and he ended up flat on the bed, moaning up a storm. He tried to catch his breath, but Patrick continued his relentless erotic conquest of his body. "Condoms are in the nightstand," Ken gasped breathlessly as Patrick's finger slipped from his body.

Ken lay on the bed, breathing deeply as he felt Patrick shift around him. He was afraid to open his eyes for fear of seeing double or even triple. He heard the drawer on his nightstand open, and then Patrick rummaging for a few seconds. Then the drawer closed and Patrick moved over him again. Patrick stroked Ken's butt and then patted his hip, and Ken shifted onto his back. He was so ready for this he could barely catch his breath. His skin was on fire. Patrick got into position, and Ken cracked his eyes open, surprised at how much he could see. Lifting his head, he watched with rapt attention as Patrick rolled the condom down his thick shaft, gasping at the thought that he was going to be filled by Patrick. Ken let his head rest back on the pillow as Patrick moved closer.

Ken felt Patrick press into his body. It had been a while for Ken, and he willed his muscles to relax. Patrick rocked slowly, and soon Ken felt Patrick slip inside him. The stretch was magnificent, and he inhaled between his teeth, hissing softly as Patrick sank partway into him. Ken gasped as his muscles throbbed, and Patrick stopped to lightly rub the spot at the base of his back. Ken caught his breath, and after a few seconds, pressed back against Patrick as a signal he was ready.

With near painful slowness, Patrick sank the rest of the way into Ken's body. Ken clenched his hands in the bedding as their bodies joined the rest of the way. Breathing as deeply as he could, Ken reveled in the sensation of joining. He felt Patrick's hips against his butt, and then Patrick loomed over him before taking him in a kiss that almost stopped his heart. Then Patrick began to move.

The breath he'd managed to briefly catch whooshed from Ken's lungs as Patrick's cock jumped and throbbed deep inside him, the small movements more erotic and intimate than being fucked through the mattress. Ken was loving the sensation of being joined with Patrick and he didn't want it to end.

In almost slow motion, Patrick pulled out of his body. Ken felt the loss like an open wound, and he whimpered until Patrick filled him once again. Ken tried to swallow his cries and ended up with the heel of his hand in his mouth as Patrick took him to nirvana over and over again. The man seemed to be some sort of magician, driving Ken to the brink of release, pulling him back, and then driving him upward again. "Patrick, please," Ken begged breathlessly as Patrick drove him toward the heights again. Patrick held his hips and drove harder than he had before. Ken rolled his head on the pillow as his body reacted with gusto. Patrick stroked along Ken's length, hand flying, gripping him hard, and Ken's body kicked into gear. Within seconds, Ken was at the precipice of passion. Patrick drove deep and hard, and Ken tumbled into passionate oblivion.

He rode waves of endorphin-induced happiness as he came hard and then floated on the afterglow, barely registering as Patrick joined him in orgasmic bliss. Ken kept his eyes closed, listening to Patrick's breathing and feeling his lover's weight resting on top of him. Ken lifted his arms away from the bedding, surrounding Patrick as he hugged him close, sharing his warmth as they both tried to catch their breaths. Ken loved holding Patrick almost as much as he enjoyed being held.

Eventually Patrick shifted next to Ken on the bed, and reluctantly Ken got to his feet, wandering into the bathroom and then returning with a towel that he used to clean them both. Then he returned to the bed and climbed beneath the covers, tugging Patrick behind him.

Ken curled next to Patrick, reveling in the last of the afterglow as he let his mind wander and tried to keep the worries at bay. Patrick held him, stroking his hair as Ken closed his eyes and let sleep carry him away.

Ken slept like the dead all night long. So much so, that when he woke alone, Ken hadn't realized that Patrick had gotten out of bed. Looking around, he found a note on the nightstand telling him that Patrick had left at about dawn. *"I'm not sure if you have explained things to Hanna and I don't want to force the situation,"* Patrick had written, and as Ken was placing the note back on the nightstand, his door opened and Hanna came into the room. While she climbed on the bed, Ken fished around on the floor for a pair of underwear and managed to slip them on as Hanna burrowed under the covers.

"What would you like for breakfast?" Ken asked, and Hanna poked her head up from the pillow.

"Mac-cheese," Hanna answered.

"We can have that for lunch. How about eggs and toast instead?"

"Okay," Hanna agreed reluctantly, squirming beneath the blankets. Ken got out of bed and pulled on a pair of jeans before lifting Hanna into his arms and carrying his giggle monster to her room. After helping her get dressed, Ken cleaned up and then took Hanna downstairs, where she ran to the front door, peering out the windows. "There are still punkmans on the porch."

Ken smiled as Hanna hurried through the house. He couldn't say how happy he was that she was acting normally. Too bad it wouldn't last.

CHAPTER
Eight

PATRICK'S heart ached as he walked the short distance from his house to Ken's, carrying a casserole dish. Over the past month or so, he and Ken had gotten closer, at least physically, and from the way Ken reacted to him, he thought Ken probably had feelings for him, which was good. That wasn't what was bothering him. It was Hanna. Over the past few weeks, he'd watched as Hanna had gone from happy to quiet and playing to sleeping all the time. He kept remembering the fun she'd had at the makeshift Halloween party, and Patrick wanted to see her like that again, but after every treatment she seemed to get worse. Now it was late in the day, and Patrick had spent much of it in his workshop trying to keep his mind off the fact that Hanna was getting yet another treatment. Ken had told him he wasn't sure how much more Hanna could take, but Dr. Pierson had told him that they had to run this course of treatments fully in order for them to work. Patrick just hoped there weren't too many more of them.

When he got to the door, he knocked softly with his elbow, and Ken opened the door with as dire an expression on his face as Patrick had ever seen. There was no need to ask how Hanna was doing because he could already see her little bald head resting on a pillow on the sofa. "Thank you, Patrick, but Hanna isn't up for food right now."

Patrick nodded, carrying the dish through the house and into the kitchen. He set down the dish, then waited for Ken before he lifted the lid. Patrick then walked to the cupboard, got out two plates, and spooned some of the pasta onto each plate before handing one to Ken with a stern look.

"I know I need to eat," Ken agreed, and Patrick pulled open a drawer and handed Ken a fork. "She's so tired all the time," Ken began as he took the first bite. "They wanted to put her in the hospital, but Hanna begged to come home. She'll probably sleep until morning, unless she starts to get sick, and then she'll be up all night, which won't help her at all." Ken set the plate on the counter and began pacing the kitchen floor. "I don't know what to do."

Patrick set his own plate aside as well and took Ken into his arms, holding him while he shook with what Patrick thought was fear.

"I have to keep her away from anyone who might have anything, because even a cold could be life-threatening. The doctor says she's hopeful that this is the worst of it, and that Hanna will start getting better soon, but I just don't see it. She gets weaker and weaker after every treatment," Ken whispered. Patrick's appetite was gone, and he understood why Ken couldn't eat much. It simply didn't seem that important.

"Daddy," floated into the room, and Ken headed for the living room. Patrick caught his eye and pointed to himself.

"Of course," Ken said, and Patrick walked into the living room, where Hanna was still resting. Patrick knelt down next to the sofa and gently lifted Hanna into his arms. She curled against his chest, resting her head on his shoulder, and Patrick thought he was going to cry right there. Walking slowly through the house, he returned to the kitchen.

"Patrick made some dinner. Are you hungry?" Ken asked, and Hanna rolled her head against Patrick's shoulder, holding him around the neck. Ken sighed softly, and Patrick pointed to the plate of food, giving Ken a stern look. He picked it up again and slowly began to eat while Patrick slowly walked with Hanna in his arms, trying to soothe her to sleep. He lightly rubbed Hanna's back as he walked, checking every so often to make sure Ken was eating.

Patrick didn't stop moving until Ken had finished his plate. Then Patrick followed Ken upstairs and into Hanna's room. Patrick rested her on the bed without Hanna opening her eyes, and Ken got her shoes off before putting a blanket over her. He retrieved Hanna's favorite pink hat from her dresser and carefully put it on her head. Quietly, they left the room, and Ken didn't say anything as they descended the stairs once again.

Back in the kitchen, Ken put Patrick's plate in the microwave, and after it was reheated, handed it to him. Patrick sat at the table finishing his lunch while Ken wandered through the kitchen, doing things that were obviously meant to keep himself busy. "What am I going to do if she doesn't make it?" Ken asked, staring at the wall as he leaned on the counter. Patrick saw Ken's shoulders bob up and down and he knew he was crying. "She's… she…." Patrick heard Ken breaking down, and he tugged him away from the counter, folding him into his arms. Ken buried his face against Patrick's shoulder and began to sob.

Patrick had no idea what to do other than try to comfort Ken. Even if he could speak, no words were going to fix this. Just like he'd done with Hanna, Patrick stroked along Ken's back to soothe him, letting Ken cry it out.

They stood together for quite awhile, until Ken's tears subsided and he moved away. "I know I'm being a baby," Ken said as he wiped his eyes. "I shouldn't be blubbering like an idiot." Ken turned away, but Patrick caught his arm to stop him. "I know. I need to be strong for Hanna and help her make the most of whatever time we have together."

Patrick wanted to tell Ken that was easier said than done, but he simply nodded and tugged Ken back into his arms. He'd been learning that if he wanted others to know what he was feeling, he needed to demonstrate his feelings rather than saying them, and right now, he desperately needed to comfort Ken, because he was being comforted as well.

"The worst part is that Hanna knows she isn't doing well," Ken explained in a whisper. "She asked me this morning how long it was until Christmas, and she asked if Santa Claus ever came early." Patrick heard Ken swallow hard. A soft knock sounded at the front door. Ken moved away from him, and Patrick signaled that he'd answer the door to give Ken a chance to compose himself.

Patrick opened the door and saw Julianne standing on Ken's porch with Todd in her arms. "Since you weren't home, I thought I'd try here," Julianne said, and Patrick motioned her inside, putting his finger in front of his lips. "Is Hanna asleep?" she asked, and Patrick nodded.

"How is she?" Julianne asked over Patrick's shoulder, and he turned as Ken approached them.

"Very tired and scared," Ken answered.

"Patrick told me yesterday that she was having another treatment," Julianne told Ken, and he nodded. "We don't mean to disturb you, but Todd's preschool class made pictures for Hanna, and I wanted to give them to you." Julianne set Todd down and pulled a sheaf of large drawing paper out of her bag, handing it to

Ken. "Todd told his class for show and tell that he had a friend who was very sick, and they made these for her." Todd looked proud of himself, and rightfully so, in Patrick's opinion. He lifted Todd into his arms and gave him a huge hug.

As Patrick held him, Todd reached over to where Ken stood and began looking through the papers. "That one's mine," Todd said, and Ken held up the picture. "It's the Haboween party," Todd explained, his eyes huge, and Patrick hugged him again.

"Thank you," Ken said to Todd, looking a bit stunned. "All of you."

"Is there anything you need?" Julianne asked, and Patrick looked to Ken, who shook his head.

"Prayer?" Ken questioned softly.

"You already have that," Julianne explained. "Are you eating? Do you need help around the house or in the yard?"

Ken shook his head. "Patrick has been helping in the yard, and much to Hanna's delight, he's been helping with a lot of the cooking. I've been known to burn water."

Patrick saw a confusing expression on Ken's face that he couldn't read, but it looked like he might have figured something out. He glanced at Julianne to see if she'd seen it too, but she didn't react and continued talking. "Don't be shy about asking for anything you need."

"Thank you," Ken answered, looking shaken and lost.

"I need to get this one home for his nap," Julianne said as she took Todd from Patrick's arms. "Tell Hanna her friends are thinking of her." Julianne walked toward the door. Patrick hurried to open it for her, and she waved good-bye as she descended the stairs. Patrick closed the door and turned around. Ken stood in the same spot, looking at the drawings in his hand, smiling as he saw pictures of crude horses and cars. Some of the drawings were mostly scribbles of color, while others were pictures where figures and shapes were definitely recognizable.

"I'll put these on the coffee table for Hanna," Ken said as he set down the drawings. Patrick wandered into the kitchen, putting away the food and making sure everything had been cleaned up. When he was done, Patrick found Ken in his studio, staring out the window into the backyard. "I've tried to paint for weeks, and nothing comes."

That was perfectly understandable to Patrick. He hadn't spent time in his shop in weeks. Patrick had finished his latest projects and hadn't started anything more.

Ken looked away and then rummaged in a set of paintings leaning against the wall, turning them around. Hanna's face greeted him from canvas after canvas. Some of them smiling, wearing her favorite pink hat. Others with her looking tired and drawn, and one painting where she was asleep, her head bald, looking small and helpless as she rested on a huge bed. "This is all I see now," Ken explained, pointing to the last portrait. "I try to see her the way she was, but I can't."

Patrick looked around for something to write on and found a pencil and a notepad from an art supplier. "*You need some rest too.*"

"I can't sleep. What if something happens to her while I'm not there?" Ken asked, almost shouting.

"*Maybe you aren't meant to see Hanna like she was. Maybe you need to see her as she is and paint that,*" Patrick wrote and then tore the page off the pad, handing it to Ken before writing some more. "*We know what happy children look like. Maybe we all need to see pictures of Hanna sick so we can understand what that little girl is going through and how hard she's fighting.*" Patrick handed the page to Ken. "*But you can't do that if you don't sleep too.*"

"Are you saying there's some plan for Hanna's illness?" Ken asked, looking almost furious.

Patrick shook his head. *"Only that maybe something good can come of it if you can show how hard Hanna is fighting. Maybe others can take heart and find courage from it. Because Hanna is one of the bravest people I have ever met in my life."* Patrick felt tears well up as he handed Ken the page. He knew he was probably reaching, but that had been how he'd felt about his music. It wasn't always happy, but helping each other through the hurt and pain of life was what people were supposed to do. He'd done it through his songs, and Ken could do it through his art. Watching as Ken read what he'd written, he saw the anger dissipate from Ken's face.

"She is courageous," Ken agreed, and Patrick walked toward the door before stopping to write one more note.

"Get some rest. You'll be able to think much clearer if you aren't so tired." Patrick handed Ken the note before clapping him lightly on the shoulder, holding Ken's gaze until he agreed; then he opened the studio door.

"I'll lie down if you lie down with me," Ken said, and Patrick nodded, extending his arm and letting Ken lead him up to his room.

Patrick kicked off his shoes before lying down on the bed. He waited for Ken to join him and then held him, stroking his hair until he fell asleep. Patrick listened to Ken breathe and watched him sleep for a while before dozing off himself. He didn't sleep long, and spent the rest of the time holding Ken, which was something he'd never get tired of.

PATRICK shut off the band saw in his workshop. He'd spent many hours cutting wooden pieces, and he'd spend days putting all the pieces together. Checking the clock, he saw he still had an hour, so he fired up the sander and got to work smoothing the edges of all the pieces. Lately, working in his shop was the only thing that seemed to calm him. He was on a mission, and after weeks without working, it felt good to be doing something.

An hour later, Patrick set the last piece aside and turned off the sander. The room became quiet, and Patrick pulled the plugs out of his ears before he did a quick cleanup, turned out the lights, and headed into the house.

In his bathroom, Patrick stripped out of his clothes and took a quick shower before dressing again and heading out for his visit to the hospital. The familiar drive went quickly, and Patrick parked and walked inside, navigating the now familiar hallways to Hanna's room. She'd been there a week, and when Patrick walked in, he saw Hanna watching television and Ken asleep in the chair next to her bed. Patrick hadn't seen much of his lover (that was how he thought of Ken now, even though he really wasn't sure exactly what they were) outside of the hospital lately, and he knew Ken hadn't been sleeping. When Hanna saw him, she smiled, and Patrick quieted her so they wouldn't wake up Ken, then bent over the bed to hug her.

"I'm feeling better," Hanna told him. They'd sort of gotten into a routine. At first Ken had asked all the normal questions for him, but now Hanna just supplied the answers. "Dr. Angie says I'm done with treatments." Hanna yawned, and Patrick nodded and hugged her again. Then he let her settle on the bed and sat down in the other chair, watching the Disney Channel with her until Ken stretched and opened his eyes.

"Have you been here long?" Ken asked in a whisper, and Patrick lifted his hand, waving it back and forth in their signal for not too long ago. Looking toward the bed, he saw that Hanna had fallen asleep, and Ken yawned and stretched as he stood up, and Patrick followed him out of the room. "She's had her last round of treatments. The doctor says there isn't anything more they can do for her right now. She believes Hanna's at the turning point, and she'll either recover now or…." Ken's voice trailed off, and Patrick didn't need him to continue with his thought. He knew exactly what Ken was saying, and he felt the fear and anxiety settle in his stomach. "All we can do now is wait," Ken added in a cracked voice.

Patrick had taken to putting a small pad and pen in his shirt pocket, and he pulled them out. *"When do they expect Hanna to be able to come home?"*

"Dr. Pierson thinks she'll be able to leave on Saturday. She wants to watch her for a few more days, and then I can bring her home. She's stronger than she was yesterday, and she's starting to eat again."

"I'll bring some mac-cheese for her tomorrow," Patrick wrote, and Ken smiled.

"Hanna will love that," Ken said with a sigh.

"You need to get more sleep!" Patrick wrote with his most nagging punctuation, and Ken simply nodded his agreement.

"I'm really tired, but Hanna needs me and I don't want to leave her alone," Ken told him, and Patrick read between the lines, knowing Ken wasn't going to leave, because if anything happened, Ken was determined to have spent every second he could with her.

"I know," Patrick wrote, meeting Ken's eyes. There hadn't been many times in Patrick's life when two words had meant so much. Patrick did know, and he understood, even if he was worried about Ken. *"I'll be here for a while. Go get something to eat and take a rest. She won't be alone."* Patrick showed Ken the note, and to Patrick's surprise, Ken agreed.

He went back into Hanna's room and sat next to the bed while Ken leaned over Hanna. "Uncle Patrick will be here for a while," he told her, and Hanna nodded, barely opening her eyes. Ken kissed her and then quietly left the room. Patrick sat next to the bed, watching the images on the near silent television for a while before turning it off and watching Hanna. He saw her reach out, and Patrick took her small hand in his. Hanna's skin seemed almost paper thin, and she seemed so fragile, he was afraid to rub. Hanna went back to sleep, and Patrick continued to sit with her. Eventually he nodded off himself.

When Ken returned, Patrick lifted his head and found Hanna stirring. Ken looked better, and he explained that the hospital had a family area where he could clean up and even lie down. Hanna's dinner was brought in on a tray, and Ken had to tell her about Patrick's promise to bring in her favorite if she'd eat her dinner. She picked at the food and eventually ate some of it. When she was done, Ken set the tray aside, and the three of them spent the next hour together.

Eventually Patrick got up to leave, kissing both Hanna and Ken good-bye. Hanna got a kick out of picking on them for kissing, but Patrick didn't mind, not one bit. As long as she got better, Hanna could pick on them for kissing for the rest of her life and Patrick would be very happy.

Patrick drove back to Pleasanton, but didn't go home. Instead, he stopped at Julianne's. The door opened like she'd been expecting him, and maybe she had. He'd been stopping most evenings after he left the hospital. "How's Hanna?" she asked, and Patrick followed her inside, writing a quick note that briefly explained what Ken had told him. "She's coming home Saturday?" Patrick nodded. "Ken's sleeping at the hospital?" Patrick nodded again. "Then it looks like we have work to do, and we'd better get things moving."

Patrick found himself back at the door before he knew what was happening. "I have calls to make, and you have work to do," Julianne said. There was nothing like getting the bum's rush from his cousin.

"Uncle Patwick!" Todd cried and launched himself into Patrick's arms for a hug as Patrick was about to turn to walk back to his car. Patrick held him while Todd told him all about his day. At least that was what Patrick hoped he was telling him—Julianne was no help when he asked her, and Todd seemed intent on talking on forever. Patrick listened and nodded until Julianne lifted Todd out of his arms, and then he continued to his car, driving off with a wave. At home, Patrick ate something quickly and spent the rest of the evening in his workshop.

Before going to bed, Patrick made a list of all the things he had to do and double-checked it by sending a few messages to Julianne. They messaged each other for a while, and then Patrick turned out the light.

Patrick couldn't get to sleep. He was worried about Hanna, and what Ken had told him. He was also worried about Ken. He hadn't slept much in weeks, Patrick knew that, and he wasn't sure how long Ken could continue on this way. Of course he desperately hoped Hanna was going to be okay. She'd been through so much already. Patrick lay in bed wondering about what he had planned, and he hoped both Ken and Hanna liked it. And more importantly, that Ken understood what Patrick was trying to say. That was what scared him the most, that Ken wouldn't get his message.

CHAPTER
Nine

KEN could barely keep his eyes open. Sitting in the chair next to Hanna's bed, he tried to stay awake, but his eyes closed on their own. He and Hanna had been waiting since that morning for Dr. Pierson to make her rounds and then sign Hanna's discharge papers. The hospital hadn't delivered lunch, so Ken had left the room briefly to bring something back for Hanna and himself from the cafeteria. If Dr. Pierson didn't make an appearance soon, he would have to make another run to get her dinner. That seemed to be fine with Hanna, who had eaten her lunch without complaint, which had been a relief for Ken. Hanna's appetite had been slow to come back. Dr. Pierson had said that happened sometimes and not to read too much into it. Ken, however, had been watching and analyzing everything to the point that he was nearly driving himself crazy.

"Daddy, can we go home soon?" Hanna asked again. She'd been dressed and ready for her trip home for a while. The only thing Ken needed to do was to get her shoes on and carry her and her things out of the hospital.

"Yes. We're just waiting for the doctor, and then we can go home." He was just as ready as Hanna to be home. He also knew that part of the lure of home was seeing Patrick on a regular basis. He'd developed deep feelings for the silent man, though he knew they needed to talk about those feelings, and Patrick deserved to hear how Ken felt. Basically, they really needed to talk. He'd told Patrick yesterday that Hanna would be coming home today, so he hadn't come up to visit. "Would you draw some pictures for me?" he asked to keep Hanna busy.

"What kind of pictures?" Hanna asked, already scrambling to get her pink art box.

"Why don't you draw a picture of all the people who have been so nice to you while you were sick?" Ken said off the top of his head, and Hanna nodded, opening the plastic box while Ken pulled out a large sheet of folded paper from one of Hanna's bags and smoothed it out on the hospital tray. Hanna got to work, and Ken leaned back in the chair again and closed his eyes.

He must have dozed off, because the next thing he knew, Hanna was calling his name, and when he opened his eyes, she'd completed a group picture. "That's our house," she explained as she pointed. "There's you and Uncle Patrick." He noticed that he and Uncle Patrick were holding hands. "There's Aunt Julianne and Todd, my friend Mary, and this is Nurse Greta and that's Nurse Paul," she explained. Ken knew there were more people, but these were the ones who had been there for them. The past few weeks had been rough, but the support both he and Hanna had gotten, both from the people who worked in the hospital as well as people they'd met, had been almost overwhelming.

"It's beautiful, honey," Ken said, looking at the surprising detail in each of the figures.

"I wanted to draw it the way you paint people," Hanna explained with a smile as she handed him the drawing. Ken carefully folded it, and Hanna sat on the bed, reaching for the television remote. She became engrossed in the television for a while. "I'm hungry, Daddy," Hanna told him.

"I'll go down and get you something," he said just as Nurse Paul walked into Hanna's room.

"The doctor just called, and she'll be up here in a few minutes," he explained. "She received an emergency call."

"Thank you," Ken said, and Hanna insisted on giving Nurse Paul a hug before he left the room. "Do you want something right now or we can stop on the way home?" Ken dug in one of the bags and then handed Hanna a packet of crackers.

"McDonald's?" she asked, and Ken sighed and nodded as Hanna took the crackers, appearing content to wait. She ate a little and watched television until the doctor walked into the room. She checked Hanna over one last time before calling for people to help Hanna and Ken out of the hospital.

"You get plenty of rest and don't try to do too much," she told Hanna before turning to Ken. "And you get some sleep and try not to worry. You look like hell, and if I have to put you in here, I will." Hanna giggled, and Ken saw the doctor wink at her. "I want to see her in my office in a few weeks. We should know more then." Ken nodded, and the doctor received a hug from Hanna before leaving the room. It was what they'd know then that frightened Ken. Hanna couldn't take many more of these treatments.

An orderly arrived right afterward, and Ken signed some papers and carried Hanna's things behind her chair as they made their way through the hospital and out to the car. Ken got Hanna loaded and her things stowed. She waved good-bye to everyone, and Ken started the car, driving away from the hospital for what he hoped, but really didn't believe, would be the last time.

"Is Uncle Patrick going to be there when I get home?" Hanna asked as Ken pulled into the restaurant.

"I suspect so," Ken answered, and he pulled into the McDonald's drive through. As Hanna told them her order through the microphone, Ken's phone jingled in his pocket. He pulled it out and saw a text message from Patrick.

"*Is everything ok?*" Patrick had texted, and Ken knew the man was worrying.

"Yes. We stopped for dinner and we'll be home soon," Ken answered and pressed Send.

"Okay. See you soon," Patrick answered, and Ken shoved the phone back into his pocket and ordered a salad. They had their food quickly, and Ken pulled the car into a parking space. He turned the car off, placed napkins on Hanna's lap, and then set out her food on the lowered arm rest. She slowly began to eat.

Ken watched as she ate a few fries and then one nugget before nibbling on the second.

"Will my hair grow back now?" Hanna asked.

"Yes," Ken answered, looking across the seat as Hanna played with her hat. "You don't have to wear the hat if you're too warm."

"I know," Hanna said, leaving the pink hat alone and eating a few more fries. "Can Mary come over and play tomorrow?"

"I don't know about tomorrow, but I'll call her mom and maybe you can play in a few days," Ken told her. "Eat some more chicken," he prompted, and Hanna picked up a nugget and took a bite before putting it down again. She ate and talked off and on for awhile. Eventually, after Hanna had eaten most of her fries and two whole nuggets, it became clear that she was done. He'd already finished his salad, and he threw the trash in the bag. Then he settled her back into her seat for the ride home.

Hanna dozed off as they ride, but she woke up as Ken slowed down when the car approached Pleasanton. "Hanna, look," Ken said as they approached the main street of town. There were Christmas lights up everywhere. The town had Santas, candy canes, snowmen, and candles on every light post. All the businesses had lights around their windows. There were swags over the street. Ken glanced in his rearview mirror and saw Hanna turn her head, looking from window to window.

"Is it Christmas? Did I miss it?" she asked as she stared out the front window.

Ken wasn't sure what was happening. "No, you didn't miss Christmas. It's still summer." Ken stopped at a traffic light, one of two in town. The entire business district had been decorated. Ken rolled down the window, and the warm summer air filled the car. The light changed, and Ken continued, driving past the decorated business district, but as they approached their corner, Ken started seeing lights on the houses—some were white, some colored. Ken turned the corner, and it looked like their entire street had been lit up. Every house was covered in decorations. Pine trees had lights strung on them. Santas in sleighs with reindeer graced green lawns. Even their own house had lights. Ken pulled closer and saw their house, covered in lights. There was a wreath in every front window, and lights hung from the eaves and porch. Candy canes lined the walk, and there was a tree on the porch covered in pink lights.

"Daddy," Hanna cried in sheer delight. She was out of her seat and nearly out the door by the time Ken parked the car across from the house. After getting out, Ken lifted Hanna into his arms as he saw a group of people who appeared to be waiting for them standing on his lawn. "Merry Christmas, Hanna," they cried in unison, and Ken felt her struggling to get down.

Hanna raced forward as Ken followed behind, looking up and down the street and then at the crowd of people on the lawn. They clapped, and Hanna squealed in delight as she stared up at the house and everyone else. Ken approached more slowly, and he saw Julianne grinning at him, as well as the neighbors he barely knew but had said hello to a few times, all smiling. As he got closer, people stepped off to the side, parting like a curtain in front of him until only one person remained: Patrick.

He didn't move out of the way, and Ken felt his gaze like a laser beam. Ken stepped closer, and everyone around him slipped away. Ken realized in a few seconds of clarity how much he hadn't seen over the last half year. He'd been existing in a near vacuum of just himself and Hanna for so long, he'd nearly overlooked the contribution of the person who'd meant the most. Ken swallowed hard as he stood in front of Patrick. "It was all you, wasn't it?" Ken said, his mind racing. "You were the one who left all those gifts for Hanna on the steps, right?" Patrick nodded and tried to look away, but Ken touched his cheek, and Patrick met his gaze. "I thought the person who left them was being nice to Hanna, and you were, but there's more than that, isn't there?" Patrick nodded again, and Ken looked all around him. "You got everyone together to do this for Hanna, didn't you?" Ken turned back to Patrick, who was standing stock-still.

"Yes, he did," Julianne stage-whispered from beside him, and Patrick threw her a quick annoyed look, but Ken knew she was telling the truth.

Never in Ken's memory had anyone been as selfless and caring as Patrick. Ken took another step forward, cupping Patrick's cheeks in his hands before bringing their lips together in a kiss Ken felt from his lips to the tips of his toes. "I love you too," Ken whispered softly, making sure those words were for Patrick only. Ken had suddenly realized that all of this, and everything that Patrick had done, was a reflection of Patrick's feelings for him and for Hanna.

Patrick smiled, and the touch of anxiety Ken had seen in Patrick's eyes shifted to pure, outright joy. Before he knew what was happening, Ken had been pulled in to a hug that nearly took his breath away. When he shifted his head so he could peer into Patrick's eyes, he was once again kissed within an inch of his life.

"Um, you're putting on a bit of a show," Julianne stage-whispered from behind him, and Ken smiled against Patrick's lips as their kiss gentled and ended. Ken grinned and stepped away, but not too far, as Patrick wound his arm around Ken's waist. "So," Julianne announced, "this is a party, and there are Christmas cookies on the porch, along with eggnog and punch. We also have plenty of munchies, and if I'm not mistaken, I understand that Santa Claus has been asked if he would come down from the North Pole for a little while." Julianne looked at the group of kids, and a cry of excitement filled the evening, with some of the younger ones jumping up and down, Hanna among them.

Christmas music began to play, and people talked as the party commenced. For the next hour, people ate, talked, and laughed. The kids played on the front lawn, with some of them peering up and down the street every few minutes, looking for Santa.

"I'm Wanda, and this is my husband Greg," an older woman whom Ken had seen walking her dogs through the neighborhood told him. "We live on the corner, and if you need anything, please let us know. Our son had cancer when he was young. We were lucky, though, just like you will be with your Hanna."

Ken swallowed. "Thank you. I guess the hardest part is the waiting and not knowing."

Wanda nodded understandingly. "Yes. It was like that for us too. But it looks like you aren't alone," she added with a smile to Patrick, "and that's what counts." A cry of delight went up from the children, and Ken looked around, wondering what was going to happen next. "They thought of everything," Wanda said as Julianne came through the group carrying a box.

"Santa can't come unless we get the tree decorated," she called out as she set down the box near the tree, and all the kids gathered around. Julianne opened it and began pulling out candy canes, lollipops, and all kinds of wrapped candy ornaments. Ken had no idea where she'd gotten them, but she began handing them out, and the kids started placing them on the tree.

Ken watched as Hanna took her turn, and as she approached the tree, Ken lifted her off her feet and she placed her candy cane high on the tree. Julianne handed her another, and she had a ball placing ornament after ornament. Other parents did the same, and soon the tree was covered in candy that had every child's eyes boggling.

"There's something coming down the street," one of the parents called, and everyone turned to watch a red convertible park in front of the house, with Santa behind the wheel.

"Merry Christmas," he called, and the kids went nuts. Santa opened his door and got out of the car, lifting a bag from the backseat before hefting it over his shoulder. He stepped partway up the walk and looked around. Ken had no idea who was in the suit, but to Hanna, along with every other kid there, this was Santa Claus. "So I understand you've all been good boys and girls," Santa said, and every youngster said "yes" almost in unison. Julianne brought one of the chairs out onto the lawn, and Santa took a seat while the kids all lined up for their chance to see Santa.

"I know exactly what I want from Santa," Ken said as he turned to Patrick. "And I don't think it's in that bag." Ken smiled, and he saw Patrick leer back and then felt Patrick tighten the hold around his waist. They wandered out onto the lawn, and Ken leaned against Patrick as Hanna slowly climbed onto Santa's lap. He saw them talking softly, and then Santa reached into his bag and rummaged before coming out with a wrapped present that he handed to Hanna. She took it tentatively, and Santa helped her to her feet. Ken saw her walk toward them. "What have you got?" Ken asked, and Hanna sat on the grass and carefully began to unwrap what looked like a shoebox. Once the paper was gone, Hanna carefully opened the box and lifted out a wooden doll cradle.

Ken knew instantly who'd made it, and as he watched all the children open their boxes, Ken realized that Patrick had made each of the gifts. There were wooden airplanes and trucks, marionettes, and for Todd, a rocking horse. The toys were beautiful, and Ken knew each of them had been made with love. As he stood with Patrick on his lawn, Ken could feel that love all around him, and for the first time in quite a while, he was able to let go of his worries and fear and relax just a bit.

The guests talked and the children played on the lawn in the glow of all the Christmas lights. Eventually, people began to drift away, saying good night, waving, and wishing each other a Merry Christmas. Santa had left after giving out the gifts, waving from his convertible. With the party quieting, Ken took Hanna inside and put her to bed, but not until she'd placed one of her dolls in her cradle.

"Thank you," Ken said to Julianne when he rejoined the small party still talking on the porch. "I can't believe all of you did this."

"It was all Patrick's idea," Julianne explained as she wrapped up the last of the food. One by one, the lights on the various houses had blinked out, and now just a few homes were still lit. She bumped Patrick's arm as she lifted a box to carry it to her car. There was another one, and Ken picked it up and followed her out. "That's the last of it," she said after Ken placed the box in her trunk, and she shut the lid. Patrick wandered down and gave her a hug.

"Good night and thank you again," Ken said as he and then Patrick were each hugged. Julianne then retrieved an already sleeping Todd from the love seat on the porch and got him into the car. With a good-bye and a wave, she drove away.

Ken and Patrick wandered back up to the porch. The chairs were back where they belonged. The candy had been picked clean off the tree by the kids, so there was very little cleanup. Even all the wrapping paper was in trash bags, sitting by the curb. Ken sat in one of the chairs, and Patrick motioned for him to wait there before rushing down the stairs. Ken watched as Patrick hurried to his house, and he saw the lights blink out.

In the darkness, Ken saw Patrick walk back across the yards until he climbed onto the porch and stood directly in front of him. "I can't believe you did all this," Ken began, motioning around him, "and I can't believe you never said how you felt."

Patrick placed his hands on his hips and glared down his nose at Ken. That single look spoke volumes.

"I know," Ken paused, "I didn't say anything either and I probably should have. But you're not exactly the most forthcoming person, you know." Patrick leaned closer. "I think we need to learn to communicate with each other better." Patrick moved even closer, and Ken held still, his gaze meeting Patrick's. "Maybe if I'd had all the facts, I could have—"

Patrick's lips met his, and Ken forgot all about talking. Wrapping his arms around Patrick's neck, Ken held him close as their lips and tongues dueled and sparred in the glow of the Christmas lights. Ken moaned softly from deep in his chest, and Patrick deepened the kiss, his firm lips taking Ken to heaven. Patrick's heady, male flavor ripped through Ken as he returned each kiss. Patrick's teeth lightly scraped his bottom lip, and Ken growled, tightening the grip around Patrick's neck in case he dared try to pull away.

"I do love you," Ken said softly when the kiss ended, leaving them both breathless. He kept his arms around Patrick's neck and saw Patrick smile, his expressive eyes with the crinkle just around the edges telling Ken everything he needed to know. He'd seen that look many times over the past few months, mostly when Patrick didn't know he was looking, but what Ken wanted to know was why he understood it so fully now. Maybe he was looking for it—and hoping for it—now. Or maybe he'd been too self-absorbed and had almost let his single-minded focus on Hanna get in the way of love.

Patrick must have seen the confusion in Ken's eyes, because he shook his head. Searching around him, Patrick found a napkin and pulled a pen from his pocket. *"You had to take care of Hanna, and at the time that was what was important. I didn't let you see how I felt because that would have interfered with what was more important."* Patrick grabbed another red napkin, after handing Ken the first. *"Hanna was what was important, not you and not me."*

"Then what changed your mind?" Ken asked as he clutched the napkins.

"Everything," Patrick wrote. *"I think I sort of realized that we were all important and that if I wanted to be a part of both your life and Hanna's life, then I better say something. And I do. More than anything."*

Ken added the napkin to the others. Then he stood up and tugged Patrick to him for another kiss. "Sometimes I think Hanna's the smart one. She's known you've been a member of our family for months now. There isn't a day goes by that she doesn't ask when Uncle Patrick is going to come see her. In the hospital, the highlight of her day—both our days," Ken corrected, "was when you came to visit."

Patrick's eyes widened in a "yeah?"

"Yes," Ken said, answering the unspoken question. Patrick reached for another napkin, and Ken touched his hand to stop him. "You don't ever have to write the three important words." Patrick tilted his head to the side, and Ken read the expression with ease. "I knew because you have that look again. You don't have to write it because you've already said it in so many ways." Ken stood up and took Patrick's hand. "I think it's time we both expressed what we're feeling." Ken moved close enough that he could feel Patrick's body heat. "There are times when words are definitely overrated, and I think this is going to turn into one of those times." Patrick nodded slowly and then stepped away. At the corner of Ken's porch, he picked up a cord and pulled the plug, plunging them into darkness as the tiny colored lights went out. Then Patrick took Ken's hand and led him inside.

The front door closed behind them, and Patrick continued leading them through the nearly dark house. The stairs loomed in front of them, and Patrick slowly began to climb, the risers creaking slightly beneath their footsteps. At the top of the stairs, Ken heard a sound from Hanna's room. Pushing open the door, he peered inside. She'd tugged off her hat and it rested on the floor. Ken came closer and saw that she'd shifted. He lightly touched her forehead, but she seemed cool and was soft to the touch. After repositioning the covers over her, Ken looked at her once again before leaving the room.

Patrick had waited in the hallway, and he took Ken's hand once again, leading him to the bedroom. Inside, Patrick quietly closed the door, and Ken stripped off his shirt, shoes, and socks, watching in the dimness as Patrick did the same. He knew the man in front of him, and Ken closed his eyes, placing his hands on Patrick's chest. He knew him and he knew his heart. Ken could feel it beating quickly in Patrick's chest, and he moved still closer, his hands sliding along Patrick's skin and around to his back. Their lips met again, and Ken held Patrick close, tilting his head into Patrick slightly.

As they kissed, Ken felt Patrick work open his belt, and moments later, his pants slid down his legs. Ken stepped out of them and felt Patrick step out of his. Then he was moving backward, Patrick's lips propelling him back toward the bed. The back of his legs hit the side of the mattress, and Ken was guided down into the bed. Ken felt Patrick climb on the bed, and his head began to spin as Patrick's naked flesh met his, chest to chest, the coarse hair on Patrick's legs tickling Ken's as their legs entwined. The roughness felt incredible, as did the way Patrick's hips fit with Ken's. They both slowed their pace, drawing out the kisses and deepening them at the same time. Ken grasped at Patrick's back, stroking his warm, sexy skin as he tightened his grip. He had no intention of letting Patrick go.

Ken shuddered as Patrick shifted above him, lips and tongue working the base of his neck. Patrick found that special spot, and Ken moaned softly, vibrating on the mattress as Patrick worked his skin. "I love you, Patrick," Ken whispered, and Patrick kissed any remaining words away before slithering down his body. Ken arched his back, hissing softly as Patrick sucked his nipples, lightly scraping the skin. Ken loved it, and he carded his fingers through Patrick's hair, pressing his face to his skin to increase the sensation. Patrick was addictive, and Ken needed to get as much of him as possible. "God," Ken groaned, and he felt Patrick smile against his skin.

Patrick slid further down his body, kissing and licking his skin. Patrick lightly tickled him with a fingertip, and it took Ken a second before he realized that Patrick was writing on his skin. Ken concentrated on what Patrick was doing, and he realized Patrick was slowly writing "I love you" on his chest. When he'd first met Patrick, Ken had wondered how he could effectively communicate, but he had quickly learned that Patrick was incredibly expressive and that he usually managed to get his point across. This was another amazing example. Ken took Patrick's hand in his, bringing it to his lips before kissing Patrick's fingers.

"I love you too, and I'll feel that for a long time. You wrote your feelings on my heart, and I'll carry them there always."

Patrick nodded, and Ken saw the smile threaten to burst on Patrick's lips. After releasing Patrick's hand, Ken cupped Patrick's cheeks and brought their lips together. Ken knew they had all night, and he intended to make advantage of it. If neither of them slept a wink, that was fine with him. He was loved. Patrick loved him, and that was all that mattered at the moment.

Patrick nipped at Ken's lower lip, and he whimpered. Then he moved away, and Ken closed his eyes as Patrick peppered his skin with licks and kisses as he worked his way down his body again. Ken's cock throbbed with each movement, and as Patrick reached his stomach, Ken held his breath in the hope Patrick would keep going. He did. Patrick licked down the side of his cock. "Yes…," Ken hissed, and Patrick licked up his entire length before sliding his lips around his head. Ken felt Patrick forcefully grip his length, lifting it away from his body.

Ken's breath flew from his lungs as Patrick took him deep and didn't stop until Ken felt the back of Patrick's throat. "Patrick, love!" Ken cried, thankful the door was closed, even though he really didn't stop to think about it much. Patrick stilled and then slowly lifted his head, his lips sliding up Ken's shaft, caressing the head before sliding off. Ken opened his eyes, lifting his head to see Patrick's sparkling eyes and mischievous grin. He wondered what Patrick had in mind next, but he didn't have to wait long to find out. Patrick opened his mouth and with almost agonizing slowness slid his lips down Ken's length. Ken wanted desperately to thrust his hips forward, to drive himself between Patrick's lips, but he restrained himself, gripping the bedding as he gave himself to Patrick.

Patrick slid his hands up Ken's chest, sucking him deep and hard, and when Patrick's touch reached Ken's nipples, Patrick tweaked both of them, sending bolts of lightning up his spine.

"You know just how to touch me," Ken gasped, and Patrick did it again. Tiny lights sparkled behind Ken's eyes, and he held his breath, wondering what else Patrick had up his sleeve. Patrick lifted his head, his lips sliding along and then off Ken's shaft. Ken groaned at the loss, but Patrick kissed away that groan. He took ownership of Ken's mouth with his tongue, and Ken whimpered and quivered as Patrick possessed him. When Patrick pulled away, Ken looked deeply into his eyes and swore he could see deep into Patrick's beautifully pure soul. The sight was almost overwhelming. Ken's mouth went dry, and he kissed Patrick again and again.

Ken felt Patrick pat his hip lightly, and he turned over. Patrick lay on top of him, his weight pressing Ken into the mattress, and Ken felt Patrick lick his neck. He knew what was coming, because Patrick had a thing for his backside. No one he'd ever been with could make Ken quiver the way Patrick could when he used his tongue… there. Ken arched upward as Patrick slipped down his back, licking a long line down his spine. As he got to the small of Ken's back, he licked small circles over Ken's skin, and Ken groaned deeply, thrusting his butt up and back into Patrick's face. Ken knew he was being completely wanton, but he wanted to be for his lover. Ken wanted to give Patrick everything he possibly could, and when Patrick cupped Ken's butt, spreading his cheeks apart, Ken groaned in anticipation. Patrick's tongue on his skin, no matter where he chose to use it, sent Ken into orbit, but when Patrick teased the top of his crack and slowly swirled his tongue over, Ken arched his back like a cat, anticipating Patrick's touch.

He wasn't disappointed, but he had to wait until Patrick was good and ready. First, he massaged Ken's cheeks, working his thumbs deep, ghosting them right next to the sensitive skin of his opening without actually touching it. Ken could barely stand it and regularly begged and pleaded for more, but Patrick seemed to have infinite patience, stripping away Ken's restraint layer by layer until he could take no more.

A swipe of Patrick's tongue over his opening made Ken whine loudly from the depths of his chest. Patrick blew on his now wet skin, and Ken threw his head back, stopping himself from howling as Patrick played his body like a fine instrument. Patrick worked the skin around his opening again and again. Ken's muscles throbbed and pulsed, begging for Patrick to do more, but he only had one speed. Never had Ken felt so loved in his life. His entire body was on fire, and each nerve approached overload. "Please, Patrick, don't make me wait any longer," Ken whispered, his throat dry, voice raspy as he gasped for breath.

Everything stopped. Patrick's hands rested on his butt, but he didn't move them. Ken peered to the side and saw Patrick staring at him. He wasn't doing anything, just looking and staring. Ken stared back and saw love shining in Patrick's eyes. He leaned forward, and Ken rolled over to meet Patrick's lips. He wanted nothing more than to feel and taste his Patrick. Ken could see there were many things Patrick wanted to tell him—that was plain by the swirl in his eyes.

"We'll talk, love, I promise you," Ken said, and Patrick nodded. Lifting his legs, Ken wrapped them around Patrick's waist, holding Patrick around the neck with his arms as they kissed. He wanted Patrick badly and so intensely that he could almost feel him inside his body already.

Patrick slid his hand down Ken's side and then over his hip and thigh before skimming over his butt. Ken stiffened when he felt Patrick press to his entrance, and soon a single finger breached his body. Ken arched his back as Patrick's finger sank deep inside him. This was what he wanted, and he gave Patrick a bruising kiss that left him with the faintest taste of blood in his mouth. Ken eased up, not wanting to hurt Patrick, as a second finger joined the first. "Yes, Patrick, more... I need more."

Patrick wouldn't be rushed, and Ken felt Patrick scissor his fingers inside him. His breath caught and he swallowed hard, whimpering softly with excitement.

The fingers inside him slipped out, leaving him empty. Ken felt Patrick shift on the bed and then heard the nightstand drawer open. Ken felt his patience slipping away, but forced himself to wait until Patrick had the condom on and had thoroughly lubed him. "Will you let me?" Ken asked, and Patrick nodded, looking a bit confused.

Ken patted Patrick's leg, and he rolled off Ken's body, resting on the mattress. Ken knelt and guided Patrick to the center of the bed. Then he straddled him, positioned his thick cock, and slowly lowered his body onto Patrick. The stretch and burn were incredible. He stopped and waited before sinking further, resting his hands on Patrick's strong chest. When his butt rested against Patrick's hips, Ken sighed and closed his eyes. The feelings were overwhelming, and he had to take a little time to adjust. Then, slowly, he lifted his body, Patrick's cock pulling in him as it slipped from his body. "Damn, Patrick, with you I never know which is better—out"—Ken held himself with Patrick just inside him—"or in." Ken sank down onto Patrick's cock and felt him throb and twitch inside him. "You always feel right, like you were made for my body." Patrick nodded enthusiastically, and Ken took that as agreement as he lifted his body once again.

Ken could feel Patrick shuddering beneath him, and he knew he was driving Patrick out of his mind, which was good, because Patrick always did that for him. Ken watched as Patrick's eyes began to boggle, and he clenched his muscles, taking Patrick deeply once again. If it hadn't seemed too incredibly spectacular, Ken probably would have smiled at the way Patrick's stomach tightened and his mouth hung open. Ken loved that he could do that to Patrick.

Swaying his hips, Ken rode Patrick like a horse, with small movements that caused Patrick's cock to rub along that spot inside in each and every time. So it took him by surprise when Patrick surged forward, holding him close as he flipped them on the bed. Ken knew Patrick would have growled if he could. Instead, he heard a breathy sound, and then Patrick was driving mercilessly into him. Ken could tell that Patrick's control had been stripped away. The bed rocked, and Ken clutched the blankets as Patrick drove him to heaven. There was no stopping him. Thank God, because stopping was the last thing Ken wanted. Patrick snapped his hips, driving his cock deep, and Ken writhed on the bed, trying to maintain the last of his control. He wanted the pressure and excitement that were already building in his body to last, so he refrained from stroking himself, but Patrick had other ideas. Patrick enclosed Ken's cock in a firm grip, and Ken clamped his eyes closed, placing himself completely in Patrick's care as his release continued to build.

"Patrick, I can't wait...," Ken said breathily, and Patrick stroked harder, tugging him to the pinnacle of desire before pushing him over the edge. Ken cried out and came all over himself as he felt Patrick throb deep inside him.

Ken was wrung out and bathed in sweat as he collapsed onto the bed. He could barely move, and he saw Patrick's eyes roll back into his head just as he tugged Patrick down onto him. Ken held Patrick close as they breathed softly into each other's ears. Ken desperately needed to catch his breath, and from the sound of things, Patrick did too, so Ken closed his eyes and held onto Patrick. Ken was so wrung out, he thought for a few seconds that he was going to nod off, but then Patrick shifted and got out of the bed. Ken wondered where he was going until he heard the water start, and then Patrick returned, extending his hand, and Ken got out of bed as well, following Patrick.

They stepped under the water, and Ken's legs felt wobbly. Luckily, Patrick held him tight as the water washed over them. Patrick kissed him softly, tenderly, and then reached for the soap to begin washing him. His touch was so gentle and caring that Ken closed his eyes and soaked in every sensation. This was almost too good to be true. Patrick was an incredibly wonderful man, and the fact that he loved him was a little heady for Ken. This man loved him, and Ken felt the same way. He was passionately in love with Patrick.

Ken stepped under the water to wash off the soap, and then it was his turn. Ken laved all the attention and care on Patrick that he deserved. This wasn't about sex, but true intimacy and simple love. Ken caressed Patrick's chest and shoulders, stroking the hard muscles before continuing to Patrick's legs and back. He explored the planes and angles of Patrick's body as though it were the first time he'd done this. Everything seemed new, and Ken desperately needed to revel in it.

Patrick rinsed off, and Ken stopped the water before getting out and handing Patrick a towel. They dried off with grins on their faces, and after hanging up the towels, they turned off the light and left the bathroom. Patrick climbed into bed, and Ken leaned over to kiss him before putting on his robe. "I'll be right back," he said and then left the room, closing the door quietly behind him.

In the dimly lit hall, Ken made his way to Hanna's room, hoping they hadn't disturbed her. Hanna was thankfully still asleep, looking like his little angel. After replacing the covers she'd kicked off, Ken returned to the bedroom and climbed into bed next to Patrick, who pulled him close. Patrick kissed him softly, caringly, and Ken returned it, his eyes already closing. He didn't have any illusions that everything would be all right. He didn't know what was going to happen with Hanna, but he felt safer knowing Patrick was there. Ken hugged Patrick close, curling to him in the cool room as sleep overtook him.

Ken woke hours later. Peering at the clock, he saw it was three in the morning. He stared at the ceiling, listening to Patrick's slow, rhythmic breathing for a while before carefully getting out of bed. There was no way he was going to fall back to sleep, so he slipped on an old pair of sweats and a T-shirt before quietly leaving the room. Ken checked on Hanna and then continued down the stairs to his studio. On nights like this, when he couldn't sleep, he usually worked. It seemed to be the only way to get his mind to let go. After turning on the lights, Ken stood in the center of the room and looked around. He'd begun a number of canvases over the past few months and he'd finished some of them, but there was one that was playing in his mind. It was the portrait of Patrick he'd begun all those months ago. He'd thought he'd finished it, but after last night, he knew there was something missing. As he searched for the canvas, he carefully placed all the ones he'd done of Hanna together. At the bottom of those, Ken located the canvas he wanted and set it on his easel. He was right. The eyes weren't what he wanted. Those had come to him early, and now he realized they were missing a certain light that should definitely be there. He opened the drawers and began placing tubes of paint on the table beside him and then grabbed his palette and a detail brush.

Before long, Ken was deep into his work. The small touches he saw in his mind made the painting come alive. Ken stepped back after adding the tiniest reflection of light into Patrick's eye and smiled. He could see him on the stage, singing his heart out, giving it everything he had and loving every second of it. Last night, Ken had seen the joy he wanted, and while he'd been close in the original work, only now was he able to finish it.

Ken lifted his gaze from the canvas as a sound from outside the room reached his ears. Patrick stood in the doorway, wearing only jeans, slung low on his hips. Ken set his brush aside, looking over his work one last time. His first art teacher had always said greatness came when you learned when to stop, and Ken knew he was done. Motioning Patrick over, he hoped to see that his lover liked it. Patrick stepped into the room, and Ken turned the easel so Patrick could see the painting.

Patrick stood stock-still as soon as he saw it. Ken had thought Patrick might be surprised, but he simply stared until tears ran down his cheeks. "I hope you like it," Ken said softly, and Patrick nodded, wiping his cheeks with the back of his hand. "I started it a while ago, but was only able to finish it tonight." Patrick nodded, still staring at the painting. Ken found a tablet and pencil, handing them to Patrick. "Please tell me what you think."

"*How did you know?*" Patrick wrote, his hand shaking a bit.

"I've watched you for months, but mostly I listened to your music." Ken stepped closer, wiping another tear that ran down Patrick's cheek. "I didn't do this to hurt you, and I'll destroy it if you want me to." That idea hurt, but he would if that was what Patrick wanted.

"*Please don't,*" Patrick scribbled, shaking his head vehemently. "*It's beautiful,*" Patrick wrote, and the knot in Ken's stomach released.

"I did others of you," Ken explained as he slowly walked to the far wall, turning around four more canvases, one life-sized. Patrick's eyes widened when he saw the painting of himself barefoot, wearing only a pair of jeans. "That's how you look when you're working outside," Ken explained as he pointed to the full-size portrait. "I wanted to capture you when you seemed happiest." Ken had thought a number of times of painting a nude of Patrick, but he wouldn't do that unless he sat for him. There were other portraits, some completed, most in various stages of work.

"*Is this how you see me?*" Patrick wrote on the tablet, and Ken smiled.

"Sometimes," Ken admitted. "I think it would take me a lifetime to capture everything about you, and by the time I did, you'd have changed." Ken moved close to where Patrick stood still looking at the paintings. "But I want to try, if you'll let me." Patrick nodded, and Ken smiled, moving into Patrick's arms. "Good. I'm going to hold you to that," Ken said happily as he squeezed Patrick's waist tightly, resting his head against his chest.

When they separated, Patrick motioned toward the other canvases. "Those are mostly the pictures I've done of Hanna," Ken explained, turning around the ones he'd done of her before she'd become ill. The later ones broke his heart, and he wasn't sure he could look at them right now. They'd been therapeutic to paint, but looking at them now was difficult. Maybe he could really look at them once he knew....

Patrick wandered slowly through the studio, looking at each of the paintings as Ken cleaned up. Once he was done, Ken saw him pick up the drawing Hanna had done in the hospital. Patrick looked at it for a few seconds, smiling. Patrick pointed to himself, and Ken nodded. "She loves you a lot." Patrick put his hand over his heart, and Ken knew he was saying the feeling was mutual.

Patrick yawned, and Ken followed right behind him. He turned out the light and took Patrick's hand, leading him back through the house and up the stairs. Together, they checked on Hanna once again before going to the bedroom, where they undressed and climbed into bed. Patrick held him tight, and Ken closed his eyes. There were still worries and cares, but he could lay them to rest for now.

THE next time Ken woke, it was to Patrick trying to get out of bed. Ken tightened his embrace, and Patrick settled back down. "What is it?" Ken asked, lifting his head, and he saw Patrick looking toward the door. "Is it Hanna?" Patrick nodded, and Ken thought for a few seconds. "Do you intend to be part of both our lives?"

Patrick nodded vigorously, hugging Ken more tightly.

"Then you're a part of our lives and part of our family, and I think she has a right to know if I'm seeing you," Ken explained. "Hanna has been through a lot, but I can't keep something like this from her any longer." Patrick began pantomiming, and it took Ken a while to figure out what he was trying to express. But about the time Ken began to understand what Patrick was trying to say, he heard footsteps in the hall and then his door opened.

Hanna walked into the room, and Patrick buried himself under the covers as Hanna jumped onto the bed and then stopped, looking at the lump on the far side of him. "Who's that?" she asked, pointing, and Patrick lowered the covers. "You and Uncle Patrick had a sleepover?"

"Yes, and I think Uncle Patrick and I are going to have more of them. Is that okay?" Ken asked, looking into Hanna's big eyes.

"Is he going to live with us like Mark did?" Hanna asked, shifting nervously from foot to foot. "'Cause I don't want him to go away like Mark did." Hanna crossed her arms over her chest as she walked around the bed to where Patrick was still hiding. She stood right in front of him, glaring at Patrick. "Do you promise?" Hanna asked incredibly seriously. Patrick lifted his head and nodded to her. "Cross your heart?" Hanna said, making lines on her chest.

Ken heard Patrick's hands rub inside the covers and he knew he was making the same movements. Hanna grinned and then ran back to his side the bed. "Does this mean I'll have two daddies again?"

Ken grinned as Patrick kicked him under the covers. "How about you continue to call him Uncle Patrick for a while? He and I have lots we need to talk about, but we wanted you to know that he and I love each other, and we both love you very much." Ken felt his throat clench as he gave Hanna a hug. "Now go on and get dressed, and we'll meet you downstairs to get something to eat."

"Okay, Daddy," she said before leaving the room.

Ken turned to Patrick. "We have about five minutes to get dressed before she'll be back in here," Ken warned with a wink, and Patrick shot out of the bed and pulled on his clothes. Ken couldn't stop laughing as Patrick practically leapt into his underwear and jeans. Ken dressed as well and was able to get his teeth brushed before Hanna burst back into the room.

"I'm ready," she exclaimed, and Ken lifted Hanna into his arms. After taking Patrick's hand, Ken led his family downstairs to make breakfast. "Daddy, am I going to get sick again?" Hanna asked as they entered the kitchen.

"I hope not, honey," Ken answered, setting her down and looking at Patrick. "Dr. Pierson thinks there's a chance you'll be fine, and all we can do is make sure you rest and eat well, so Uncle Patrick and I are going to make your favorite breakfast."

"Mac-cheese," Hanna said with a giggle.

"Not for breakfast," Ken said, whisking her off her feet and into his arms. "But maybe later, if you're good." Ken didn't have answers, and as much as he wished he did, he couldn't see into the future. He did know that he could make the most of the time he had, be that weeks, months, or, "Please, God…," years.

Epilogue

"KEN, where are you? I'm going out of my mind. Please, for God's sake, call me," Phillip, his agent, pleaded in his voice mail. Ken deleted the message after hearing it as he walked naked to the bathroom in their hotel room, dropping the phone on his jacket. He'd call Phillip back a little later.

Ken started the water in the shower and stepped under the spray, pulling the curtain closed behind him. He reached for the soap and began cleaning up as he heard the bathroom door open, and then the curtain was pushed aside and a beautifully naked Patrick stepped into the shower with him. "I thought you were getting dressed," Ken said, but he'd be damned if he intended to complain. So what if they were a little late. Patrick kissed him as his hands wandered all over Ken's skin. Well, a lot late. Phillip would probably come unglued, but Ken couldn't find it in himself to care, not right now. Ken moaned softly and held Patrick tighter as wet skin pressed to slippery wet skin. Ken loved the way Patrick felt, wet or dry. Granted, there was something about wet that really got him going. Maybe it was the way Patrick's chest slid over his, or the way his soapy hands slid over his skin. Somehow Ken figured it was an "all of the above" thing. "Patrick," Ken said, chuckling as his lover's gentle touch tickled along his ribs. He squirmed to get away, but Patrick tightened his grip and firmed up his caresses.

Patrick gripped his butt tightly, and Ken groaned softly in his lover's ear, pressing back into the touch to let Patrick know exactly what he wanted. Before Ken knew what was happening, he'd been whirled around and pressed against the tile. "That's it," Ken encouraged as he waited. Sometimes Patrick simply slid into him, stretching and filling until Ken screamed at the top of his lungs. Ken had told Patrick once that being silent did have its advantages, because Ken never knew what to expect, and he liked it that way. Ken's cheeks were spread, and he waited, legs shaking in anticipation, but nothing happened.

Ken was about to turn and look when he felt warm water shoot against his opening, and a few seconds later, it happened again, this time followed by Patrick's tongue and lips. "Jesus, what are you doing to me?" Ken pressed against the tile, his legs shaking so hard he wasn't sure how much longer he could stand up. When Patrick speared him deep, Ken groaned and spread his legs further. He was expecting more of the same, but what he got was Patrick pressed to his back, cock pressing inside him. "Yes!" Ken cried as Patrick slid inside him.

Patrick didn't slow or stop, pressing inside him in one long, slow movement. By the time Ken felt Patrick's hips against his ass, he was breathing like a racehorse and already halfway to coming, and neither he nor Patrick had touched his dick. Ken was afraid to stroke himself, because he'd be coming in seconds, so he pressed his hands flat against the tile and braced himself for whatever Patrick had in mind. Patrick's patience in these situations always got him going, and today was no exception. Ken had often thought his lover was some sort of saint, because he always seemed to have the most amazing control, and even when Ken felt as though he was going to fly apart, Patrick grounded him and then drove him to heights he'd never imagined. And he was doing just that right now.

For a second, Ken thought Patrick might have fallen asleep; he simply wasn't moving. Then he withdrew, agonizingly, excruciatingly slowly. Ken wanted to pull away so he could plunge himself back onto Patrick's shaft, but he knew that would only make Patrick go slower and tease him more. Patrick did this for him, and it was Ken who always benefited. Once, Patrick had put off his climax for so long that when he did drive Ken over the edge, he'd damned near passed out from sensation overload. "Please, Patrick, don't make me wait."

The only answer he got was a pat on the hip as he was slowly filled again. Ken knew exactly why Patrick was doing this, and he had to let him. Ken had been a nervous wreck for days, and this was Patrick's way of mellowing him out. When Patrick picked up his pace, Ken felt as though his eyes were ready to roll to the back of his head. Before, Patrick would slow down again, but this time he picked up more speed, and Ken stroked himself, resting his other arm on the tile. His breath coming in short pants, Ken tried to hold out as long as he could, but Patrick was in control, and Ken quickly felt the pressure building from the base of his tingling toes. The sensation shot up his legs, filling his entire body until he could hold it in no longer. With a loud cry, Ken shot come all over the wall of the shower, and moments later, he felt Patrick filling his body, each throb of Patrick's cock making him shiver and shake.

Patrick wrapped his arms around Ken's chest, holding the two of them together, and Ken leaned back and turned his head, and Patrick kissed him sloppily until he slipped from Ken's body. Then Ken turned around, and Patrick hugged him close. Actually, that was the only thing that kept him on his feet.

They'd probably used all the hot water for the entire hotel by the time Patrick had washed him thoroughly and turned off the water. Stepping out of the shower, they dried themselves quickly before moving to their room to get dressed.

Ken checked his phone and found four more messages from Phillip, so he took mercy on him and called before getting dressed.

"Where have you been? I've been worried sick. The opening is in two hours, and you haven't brought over the last painting yet. The gallery owner is coming unglued. They need to hang the piece but they haven't seen it." There were times when Ken wondered if the man ever took a breath, and now Ken had proof he didn't.

"Calm down. Patrick was just making sure I was good and relaxed for the show tonight. We're getting dressed, and we'll be at the gallery in half an hour with the painting," Ken explained as he watched Patrick pull on his tuxedo pants. "The longer you keep me on the phone, the later we'll be."

"Okay, just get here as soon as you can okay? You know I love ya," Phillip added before disconnecting the call. Ken chuckled as he tossed the phone on the bed and began getting dressed.

"*It's a shame you have to put clothes on,*" Patrick signed, and Ken snickered.

"I don't think the gallery would appreciate me showing up naked. They might not mind you being naked, though. But I'd have to kill anyone who looked at you, so it's probably best if we both finish getting dressed before Phillip busts a gut."

"*If you're sure,*" Patrick added with a smirk that made Ken smile. Patrick had been taking lessons in sign language for months now. Ken and Hanna had gone with him. A whole world had opened up for Patrick, and what Ken had found was a whole new side to the man he loved. Not only was Patrick great as the strong silent type, he was also incredibly intelligent, something

Ken had always known, but it had blossomed now that Patrick could communicate with the world again.

"I'm very sure," Ken said as he swatted Patrick's butt. "You're mine and you always will be." Ken punctuated his sentiment with a kiss, feeling a little loopy when it was over. "Now, we're leaving in five minutes. And remember, the sooner we get there, the sooner this whole thing will be over."

"*Amen*," Patrick signed, and Ken couldn't help smiling again at the leer on his lover's lips. Ken kissed the leer away before tying his bow tie and putting on his jacket.

"How do I look?" Ken asked, and Patrick signed something. "I don't understand," Ken said. Patrick signed again, and Ken grinned. "I understood the first time—I just wanted you to say I was hot again." Ken ducked away from Patrick's gentle swat and put on his shoes before checking himself in the mirror one last time. Then he gathered the wrapped canvas, and they left the room, heading for the elevator. The gallery was sending a limousine, and for that Ken was more than grateful. The canvas he was carrying wasn't small and he hadn't finished it in time to ship, so they'd had to transport it with them on the drive from Pleasanton to New York. Somehow, after getting into the city, they'd made it to the hotel, but neither of them had any desire to drive in Manhattan.

In the lobby, the limousine driver was waiting for them, and they got the painting inside and then rode from midtown down to the art gallery in Soho. Patrick looked out the window every few seconds like he was memorizing landmarks. "It's going to be fine," Ken reassured.

"*I haven't been out in public like this much since the accident*," Patrick confessed. "*I'm just a little nervous because people always wonder what happened.*"

"I'll handle them if they do. I just want you to have a good time and not worry about any of it," Ken said, shifting so he was sitting next to Patrick. "If you want to go back to the hotel, I'll understand." He really would,

Patrick shook his head. *"I want to be there with you,"* Patrick signed as the car stopped in front of the gallery. Ken reached for Patrick's hand, kissing his fingers softly before the driver opened the door. Ken let Patrick get out and then carefully handed him the wrapped painting, tilting it to get it to fit out the door. Once he climbed out, Ken took it, and they walked into the gallery.

"Mr. Brighton," a young man said as he held the door. "I'm Bradley, and it's a pleasure to meet you." Patrick took the painting, and Ken shook Bradley's hand. "I'm a huge fan of your work," he said with a smile as he continued shaking Ken's hand.

"Please call me Ken, and this is my partner, Patrick," Ken explained as he extricated his hand. Bradley shook Patrick's hand and then took the painting and hurried away through the gallery.

"Thank God, you made it," Phillip gushed as he hurried down the gallery's glass staircase. The whole thing looked like it floated on air. "I was about to break out the alcohol."

"It's fine, Phillip. We're here, and so is the painting," Ken soothed as his agent hugged first him and then Patrick. Phillip had visited Pleasanton a few months earlier, and when he'd seen Ken's work, he'd managed to set up this show on very quick notice. "Let's see what they've done, shall we?" Ken took Patrick's hand as Phillip gave them a tour.

"This is a relatively new gallery, and they're so very excited about showing your work," Phillip commented as he led them up the stairs.

Ken heard the gallery door open and then what sounded like a herd of elephants on the floor behind them. "Daddy," Hanna nearly screamed, and he hurried down the stairs, catching her in his arms and swinging her around. "We had the bestest time. Aunt Julianne and Uncle George took us to the Statue of Liberty, and we got to ride on a boat and everything."

"It sounds like you and Todd had a lot of fun today," Ken said happily as he shook George's hand and kissed Julianne on the cheek.

"We did, but he's pooped," Hanna explained, pointing to where Todd rested, half asleep, on his mother's shoulder.

"You should be tired too," he told her, and she smiled and shook her head.

"I should take them both back to the hotel," Julianne said, but Phillip intervened.

"The gallery has a room set up for you and the kids." He looked at Ken, who nodded.

Phillip motioned for Julianne to go first. George took her hand, and the two of them descended the stairs with the rest of their crowd following.

The gallery workers were still putting the finishing touches on the displays, so they made their way to a small room off the main gallery that had a sofa with blankets and pillows resting on the back. Julianne spread one of the blankets and laid Todd on it. He barely moved as she covered him up.

"You should stay too, to watch over him like a big girl," Ken told Hanna, and she nodded and went to sit on the other side of the sofa. Hanna lay down as well, and Ken knew she'd be asleep in minutes. Ken sat next to her, watching Hanna as she settled on the cushions. He couldn't resist stroking her silky blonde hair. It just reached her ears, but it was shiny and beautiful. Sometimes he could hardly believe he had his daughter back. She had energy and was as precocious as ever. Ken felt

Patrick's hand on his shoulder, and he met his gaze before slowly standing up. "I'll stay with them," George volunteered, and Ken nodded his appreciation before leaving the room.

They were met by Scott, the gallery manager, and Ken made introductions. "I can't tell you how honored we are to show your work," Scott said as he looked first at Ken and then at Patrick. "They're you," he said with a smile. "We placed the paintings of Patrick in the first gallery," Scott explained as he motioned them toward a medium-sized room. "Rather than grouping them close together, we placed one painting on each wall so when you come in here you're surrounded by him. The expressions are very powerful and moving. These were very obviously painted with love." Ken moved closer to Patrick, and Patrick took his hand, neither of them saying anything. The portrait of Patrick singing, and the life-sized one Ken had done, were not here. They were hanging in their home in Pleasanton. Ken had done enough paintings of Patrick, and Phillip had begged him to let him show a few, but Ken hadn't allowed any to be shown until Patrick had agreed.

"They definitely were," Ken said softly, moving a little closer to Patrick.

"Do you like it?" Scott asked him, and Ken smiled at the nervous young man.

"You did a good job," Ken said, and Patrick elbowed him slightly. Ken grinned. "Yes, I really do, and I think Patrick does as well." Ken looked to his lover, who nodded, his eyes sparkling.

"I believe they're ready in the next room," Scott said after peeking inside. "We just finished hanging everything, and if there's something you don't like, we can make a few changes," Scott explained. Ken nodded and walked into the next gallery space.

The walls were covered with the portraits of Hanna. They began when she was healthy with long, blonde hair, and showed the progression of her disease to where she was wearing hats, and then her recovery. The final one showed Hanna the way she looked today. Ken still found it hard to look at the ones of her sick, but without those, the others wouldn't be as powerful. *"They're beautiful,"* Patrick signed, and Ken nodded, his eye drawn to the works hanging on their own wall. There were two of them, framed nearly the same. One was a print of the drawing Hanna had done on her last day in the hospital, and the other was Ken's painting of the same people. Both were entitled *The Faces of Recovery*. Ken had not been willing to part with Hanna's actual drawing, so the gallery had had a single print made that would go to whoever bought Ken's work.

Ken stared at both pieces of art, his daughter's and his, hanging side by side, and he felt tears well in his eyes. Looking around, it was then he realized that he and Patrick were alone in the room. He leaned against Patrick, holding his arm as he looked at the exhibit one last time. "Is it okay?" Scott asked, breaking the silence as he and the others entered the room.

"It's beautiful," Ken said.

"There's just one thing we need to do before the evening is over," Scott explained. "I need the artist to sign her print." Scott pointed to the print of Hanna's drawing, and Ken grinned.

"I'm sure she'll be happy to," Ken said with a smile.

George came into the gallery holding Hanna's hand, with Todd on his shoulder. Hanna walked over to Ken, and he lifted her into his arms.

"So what do you have planned next?" Scott asked

Ken looked at Patrick and moved closer, feeling Patrick's arm glide around his waist. "A family portrait." Ken looked to Patrick, and he nodded.

ANDREW GREY grew up in western Michigan with a father who loved to tell stories and a mother who loved to read them. Since then he has lived throughout the country and traveled throughout the world. He has a master's degree from the University of Wisconsin-Milwaukee and works in information systems for a large corporation. Andrew's hobbies include collecting antiques, gardening, and leaving his dirty dishes anywhere but in the sink (particularly when writing). He considers himself blessed with an accepting family, fantastic friends, and the world's most supportive and loving partner. Andrew currently lives in beautiful historic Carlisle, Pennsylvania.

Visit Andrew's website at http://www.andrewgreybooks.com and blog at http://andrewgreybooks.livejournal.com/. E-mail him at andrewgrey@comcast.net.

The RANGE stories

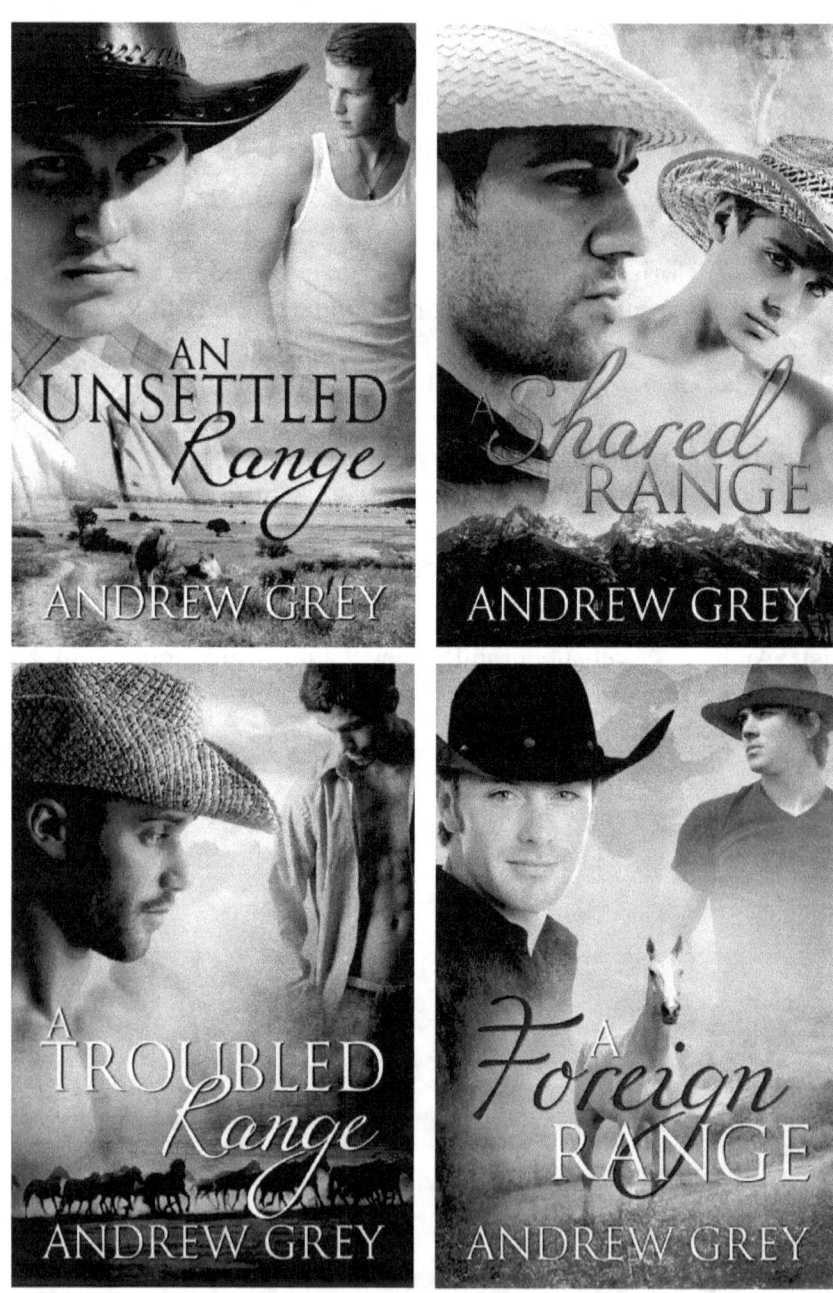

The ART stories

Now in Spanish, French, and Italian

http://www.dreamspinnerpress.com

Also by ANDREW GREY

http://www.dreamspinnerpress.com

The LOVE MEANS… stories

http://www.dreamspinnerpress.com